WHO'D WANT TO HURT
SUCH A NICE LADY?

"An eighty-two-year-old grandmother of seventeen and great-grandmother of four. Same MO, far as we can tell."

"Nobody saw anything?" I asked just for the sake of asking.

"No."

"No tire marks or fingerprints?"

"No."

Somehow, it hardly seemed fair. Here I was, in love for the first time in my life, and I should be writing poems and smelling the clover, but instead I was in the house of an old lady who'd been violated beyond human comprehension, and wondering who, what, and where the animal that did it was, if you know what I mean. I was getting mad, which wasn't a half-bad idea.

───────── ★ ─────────

Cooper's "writing is taut and suspenseful and the characters are lively and engrossing."

—*Ocala Star Banner*

"Cooper has a warmhearted winner in Kovak and the other residents of Prophesy County."

—*Booklist*

Forthcoming Worldwide Mysteries by
SUSAN ROGERS COOPER

HOUSTON IN THE REARVIEW MIRROR
OTHER PEOPLE'S HOUSES

THE
MAN
IN
THE
GREEN
CHEVY

SUSAN ROGERS COOPER

WORLDWIDE®

TORONTO · NEW YORK · LONDON · PARIS
AMSTERDAM · STOCKHOLM · HAMBURG
ATHENS · MILAN · TOKYO · SYDNEY

THE MAN IN THE GREEN CHEVY

A Worldwide Mystery/May 1991

First published by St. Martin's Press Incorporated.

ISBN 0-373-26071-7

To Don and Evin for their support,
encouragement and love

ONE

HER BODY was found by her daughter-in-law. The old lady just lay there for at least twenty-four hours after the murder, the coroner said. She had been raped and strangled. A seventy-two-year-old woman. What this world is coming to, I swear to God! As head of the Prophesy County Sheriff's Department's Homicide Unit, I was called in.

Head of the you-know-what was one of those fancy titles signifying nothing. I got the title five years ago when Barnie Littlefield shot his wife Mavis. I investigated and Barnie handed me the gun and I took him in. That, coupled with the fact that I was the only one, including the sheriff, who had kept his lunch at the scene of the big wreck out on Interstate 12 around the same time, got me the title.

What the sheriff didn't know, and what I didn't tell him, was that Barnie had been standing over his wife's body saying "That's the last time I'm eating her meat loaf" and holding a still-smoking Saturday night special. He was drunk as a skunk and the judge eventually let him off, saying as long as Barnie didn't remarry, he wasn't a threat to anyone, which I figured was something the single and widowed ladies of the county should be aware of.

And the incident on Interstate 12—well, I've always had this cast-iron constitution. Think it came from living with my mama for the first eighteen years of life. A lovely lady and a talented seamstress, but Daddy used to joke about paving the driveway with her biscuits and using the gravy as putty. If it wasn't brown and white, Mama didn't know it was food. I also used to eat worms for extra money from grade school through my hitch in the Air Force. I'd bet somebody I'd eat a whole worm; they'd say I wouldn't; I would, and I'd take their money with a smile on my face and a worm in my stomach. The wreck on Interstate 12 had made me want to cry, but not upchuck.

Taking in Barnie Littlefield for the murder of his wife had been my first and last duty under the lengthy moniker until Mrs. Olan (Beatrice) Munsky was found raped and strangled.

Mrs. Munsky's son LeRoy and his wife Anna had been over to Mrs. Munsky's as usual on Sunday after church for dinner. They'd had ham, potato salad, baked beans, deviled eggs, and biscuits, a fact confirmed by Mrs. Anna Munsky, her husband, and the autopsy. The county coroner had said, in what passed for him as humor, that if the rapist hadn't killed her, her diet sure would have.

The son and daughter-in-law left her at three that afternoon but talked to her on the phone that night around seven-thirty to remind her that the repeat of that Kojak movie she wanted to see was on.

Mrs. Anna Munsky had called her again Monday morning but there was no answer. She figured her mother-in-law was probably out in the garden and thought no more about it. She called again that evening, but there was still no answer. By Tuesday morning, the daughter-in-law was worried that the old lady may have fallen and broken a hip and couldn't reach a phone, so she rushed over there. That's when she found the body. And that's when I was called in.

I'm usually chief deputy. Unless there's a homicide. The wife hadn't liked it much when the sheriff had made me head of the Homicide Unit. She said it was dangerous. But she had been wrong, as usual. The wife said a lot of dumb things over the years and I ended up tuning them all out. That's why it took almost two days before I realized she had left me. That was six months ago. The divorce will be final soon. Anyway, I think that's what she said the last time she called. I wasn't really listening.

The Homicide Unit for the Prophesy County, Oklahoma, Sheriff's Department consists of me, and anybody who's not busy that I can borrow. For this case, with nobody around with a garrote in one hand and his pecker in the other for me to arrest, I decided I'd probably need some help. The sheriff gave me the use of the two day deputies, Dalton Petigrew and Mike Neils. Dalton was big, ugly, and about as dumb as they come. But nice. Mike was young, eager, and irritating. Like a puppy who pees on your leg a lot. I thanked the sheriff and took what I could get.

I told Mike to get on the horn to neighboring counties for any recent crimes of a similar nature and had Dalton stand guard over Mrs. Munsky's house. I drove him up there in my unmarked squad car and dropped him off, telling him not to let anybody in, and that included Mr. and Mrs. LeRoy Munsky. He nodded his head, smiled and sat down on the steps. Not that much was going to happen at Mrs. Munsky's. It was one whole day since the body'd been found, and the house had been swept for prints and clues and the body was long gone, but having Dalton stand guard made him happy and kept him out of my hair.

I decided to canvass the neighborhood myself, it being not much of a neighborhood to canvass. Old Mrs. Munsky had lived in the first place up the hill on Mountain Falls Road. It was a regular old farm that had been in her husband's family for three generations. The farm, all 750 acres of it, with Jennifer Creek running through the back of it, took up all of the Falls side of road. Mr. David Perry lived across the road and about a hundred feet down from the entrance to Mrs. Munsky's farm. I figured if anybody saw anything, it would have to be Mr. Perry.

I had never met David Perry, but I heard a lot about him when he moved here from New York City. An artist. But he'd been here in Prophesy County for three years now without any trouble.

I turned the car in the turnaround in front of Mrs. Munsky's house and drove back down the long driveway to Mountain Falls Road and made the immediate sharp turn into Mr. Perry's drive. He was just getting out of his car as I drove up, a suitcase in his hand.

"Mr. Perry," I called out.

He turned and looked at me. Tall, skinny, with a beard. Wearing jeans and a T-shirt and sandals. He didn't have "artist" tattooed on his forehead, though.

"Yeah?"

"I'm Milton Kovak, Prophesy County Sheriff's Department. Need to ask you some questions about Mrs. Munsky."

"Who?"

"Mrs. Munsky." I pointed across the road. "The lady that lives at the farm over there?"

"Oh. The old broad."

"Yes, sir. Have you heard what happened?"

He hefted his suitcase and started for the front of his house. "Look, I've been out of town. Okay if we go inside for a minute? It's hot out here."

I followed him inside, noting the interior matched his outfit. The tune to the old song "Streets of Laredo" kept going through my mind. "You can see by my outfit that I'm an artist too." The wife always said I had a plebeian sense of humor. I think she read that in the *Reader's Digest*.

The interior was filled with light from undraped windows and a skylight. Stacks of paintings were piled in the corners and the room smelled of turpentine. The living room/studio was furnished with an old couch partially covered with an Indian print bedspread, a dilapidated easy chair draped with what probably used to be a brightly colored crocheted afghan. It was now faded shades of orange, brown, and a dark gray that had probably been black at some point. There was an old hutch with doors top and bottom, one top door hanging partially open. Inside, I could see jars and cans of paints and other artist-type equipment. A coffee table in front of the couch was stacked with old newspapers and magazines. The room looked comfortable.

"So, what's the problem, Officer Kovak?"

"Chief Deputy Kovak, actually, but just call me Milt. Everybody does."

Perry smiled and extended his hand, introducing himself as if I didn't know who he was. Which I supposed was polite.

I told him about the murder and he seemed genuinely surprised. "No shit? Jeez, that's awful! Right across the street? An old lady like that?"

"Any chance you saw anything, Mr. Perry?"

He shook his shaggy head. "Naw. Sorry. I went out of town on Friday, left around noon. Just now got back. You saw me pull in."

I asked a few more questions, for record-keeping sake, thanked him, and left for the next place.

One eighth of a mile from the entrance to Perry's place was the entrance to Billy and Coral Moulini's mountain-cabin chateau. The Sheriff's Department had been notified by Billy Moulini's secretary back in May that the Moulinis would be spending the summer in Sweden this year and would not be lending the cabin to anyone without first notifying the department. We had not been notified about this weekend, but I'd call Mike from Mrs. Munsky's place and have him check with Moulini's secretary anyway.

The fourth and last place on Mountain Falls Road, before it went steeply downhill into the flood-prone area around the Falls itself, where not even city fools had dared to build, was a place I knew well. The wife and I had attempted to buy it eight years ago. Well, I had attempted to buy it. She hated the house. The entrance was a gate between two leaning newel posts surrounded by tall oaks and scrub pine that led a quarter of a mile through heavy foliage to a clearing where the house stood. And what a house.

I had studied its history while attempting to seduce the wife into agreeing to buy it. And that had worked about as well as any other seducing I'd tried to do with her. It had originally been built in the 1920s as a five-room dwelling; a living room, dining room, and kitchen downstairs; two bedrooms and a bath upstairs. The bedrooms and bath were over the dining room and kitchen, with the stairway leading from the living room, against the common wall to the kitchen, up to the hallway. A door led from that hallway to the flat roof of the living room. Unusual for this area, the house was built of stucco, which reminded me happily of the time I'd spent at White Plains in New Mexico while in the Air Force.

It had originally been built in an L shape, with the kitchen extending lengthwise at the back of the house beyond the dining room in the front, and the living room running the full width of the house, front to back. The second owners had added a master bedroom and bath, tacked onto the kitchen, running the width of the house parallel to the living room. They glassed in the area between the new bedroom and the dining room, which would have made a nifty little study or nursery or something, backing up to the kitchen, turning the house into a rectangle.

The third owner had added a sunroom off the living room at the back and enclosed the extension of bedroom and sunroom with a screened-in porch off the kitchen. I think these were the same people who added the screened-in porch to the front. Seems likely. The fourth owner, far and away the craziest, had added a room onto the second floor that extended the width of the house, from the sunroom to the bedroom, walled totally with windows, except for the small area that connected to the upstairs bedrooms. A pair of French doors led out to the roof of the living room.

That's the way the house had looked when the wife and I first saw it. She called it a crazy house. When I exclaimed about the great room of windows on the second floor with its spectacular view of a green valley and twin peaks beyond, with a dip between the peaks where you could see all the way to Tejas County, the wife had said, "Oh, yeah? And who's gonna clean these windows? You?" Which had been the end of the discussion.

The gate was open when I pulled up to the road leading to the house. I drove on up and saw a few new additions. Some I already knew about. Like the new three-car garage with the apartment above it. The people who bought the house instead of the wife and me had added that to keep his mother from actually *living* with them, along with a deck in back that ran the full width of the house. But those people had sold it and the house was now on its sixth owner, Jerry and Laura Johnson. The Johnsons had added a corral, horses, and kids. Two kids, a boy of about seven and a girl of about five, stood inside the corral, both holding the reins of a pony and arguing. I parked the car and walked up to the screened-in front porch and knocked.

The door of the house opened and a woman of about thirty-five peeked out at me. "Yes?" she asked.

I explained again who I was. Her eyes darted quickly from me to her children out at the corral. I showed her my badge and ID. She walked across the porch and opened the door a crack and took the ID out of my hand, looking from me to the picture and back again.

"Just a minute, please." With quick looks at her children and at me, she went back into the house and into what I knew was the living room. I could see her through a window, dialing and then talking on the phone. In a minute, she was back, a smile on her face. "With what happened down the road, you can't be too careful," she said.

I nodded in agreement. She was tallish and on the skinny side, wearing blue jeans too old and too proud to wear anyone's name on the butt, and an old and worn khaki shirt with the buttons misbuttoned, exposing a part of one naked breast. Her hair was almost black, thick, curly and unruly, with streaks of gray, hanging well past her shoulders. Her skin was fair with freckles. Her hands, I noticed when she offered one for me to shake, were workworn with the fingernails bitten down low. When she smiled, there was a dimple in her left cheek. And her eyes were blue, sort of. More like turquoise. With black lashes and brows. She wore no makeup and she was barefooted. She was one of the sexiest women I had ever personally seen.

"Come on in," she said, leading me into the house. I followed her through the entryway into the living room, looking around as I did. The house had been empty when the wife and I had looked at it eight years earlier. I had often thought it was best we hadn't bought it because I couldn't reconcile this house with my wife's taste in furniture, which ran to French provincial with a lot of foofaraws. The Johnsons' living room looked like it should have. The hardwood floor was polished to a high shine, and American Indian throw rugs were scattered on it. The rattan couch had seen a lot of use and there was an easy chair that looked mighty comfortable. There were several more chairs and some little beanbag-type ones that would fit the rear end of a child, and I had to walk carefully over the dolls and trucks and pull toys scattered on the floor.

There was a lot of artwork on the walls, mostly framed posters of art exhibits in one place or another, the kind you can buy at the galleries you find in shopping malls. There was an old three-tiered round table by the front window with a god-awful antique lamp on the top tier. But all in all, the place was comfortable looking.

A baby of about eighteen months was standing by the ottoman that matched the easy chair, tearing a packet of cigarettes to shreds. Mrs. Johnson scooped the baby up in one arm, grabbed the cigarettes with the other and answered the baby's unintelligible (to me) question with a laugh, and "No! Adam's not going to smoke! Nasty!"

She indicated the easy chair to me and sat down on the couch, perching the baby on one knee while deftly lighting a cigarette with a kitchen match, one-handed. She blew the cigarette smoke away from Adam but he leaned toward it, trying to catch it.

"What can I do for you, Deputy Kovak? No!" she said to the baby. "Oh, all right, back to prison for you, young man." Holding the baby like a sack of potatoes, she carried him to a playpen and deposited him amid an army of stuffed animals.

Coming back to the sofa, she said, "I'm sorry. What's a mother to do, and all that!" She laughed. It was a deep laugh, throaty. I found myself smiling like an idiot. "I suppose it's about poor Mrs. Munsky. I heard about it on the radio. God, it's just awful!"

I shook myself mentally and asked if she'd seen anything unusual on Monday morning, the day and approximate time the coroner had decided upon.

"Monday. Monday. God." She shook her head. "What's today? Wednesday? They all run together, I'm sorry—wait! Monday? I'm not sure, but . . ." She sat excitedly on the edge of the sofa. "Can you call the electric company and find out when that transformer blew? The one at the end of our drive. That could have been Monday."

I went to the phone and dialed the County Electric Utility, identified myself and asked the question. The call had come in at 11:05 A.M. Monday.

When I told Mrs. Johnson what the Electric Utility had confirmed, she grew even more excited. "Oh my God! I may have seen him!"

"What?" I got excited too.

She leaned toward me, unknowingly exposing even more of her seminaked breast in her excitement. "There was a big bang and the lights all went out. The older two kids were at vacation Bible School. Just Adam and I were here. My husband was working . . ."

"Where's that, Mrs. Johnson? Where your husband works?"

"Oh, he's a salesman for Swensen's Farm Machinery in Longbranch." I wrote that down in my book. "Anyway, I called the utility and told them. I figured it was a squirrel. It's happened twice before. They get in the transformer, chew on something they're not supposed to, and boom, there goes the squirrel and the transformer. So I took Adam and a lawn chair and walked down to the end of our drive to the road to wait for the utility truck. Wanted to make sure they didn't just go on by. They do that sometimes. I waited hours once... Anyway, I heard a car coming up the rise, sounded awful, thought it must be the truck, what with the county cutbacks and all—anyway, it wasn't, it was this old car with a man in it I didn't recognize."

"Can you describe him? Or the car?" I cut in. As exciting as her story was, I had a hard time concentrating on it. I kept hoping she'd sit back so I wouldn't have such a good view down her misbuttoned shirt.

Concentrating on a description of car and driver, she closed her eyes and took a deep breath. Which gave me the opportunity to stare all I wanted. Which was a lot. She was silent a moment and then said, with her eyes still closed, "The car was old. Bad muffler. Big. Like about a seventy model Chevy Impala. Green with rust stains. Black vinyl roof, coming up in places. Rotted like. The man inside was about thirty, I couldn't tell how tall, but he looked on the skinny side, had blond hair, straight and stringy, dirty hair; wearing sunglasses, an orange gimme cap, and a black T-shirt. He looked right at me..." Her turquoise eyes opened wide. "Oh, God! He looked right at me! But then I heard the utility truck coming up behind him and didn't pay any more attention. If they hadn't come right then..." She shook herself and stood up.

Matter-of-factly, she said, "Well, that doesn't bear thinking about, does it?"

"You didn't happen to notice the license plate, Mrs. Johnson?" I asked, also standing.

She shook her head. "No. I'm sorry."

I smiled. "Don't be. You just gave a real good description. I'll have an APB put out on this guy. You willing to sit through a line-up if we find any suspects?"

She shrugged. "Sure. I want this guy off the street as much as you."

She walked with me out to the front porch. "Thanks again, Mrs. Johnson," I said. "I'll keep in touch."

She smiled and I went weak in the knees. "You do that, Deputy. Let me know if you need me."

I waved, got in the car, and managed to turn it around. I noticed an antique VW van in front of the three-car garage. Blue and white. Original paint job. I smiled to myself. I've always had this theory about Volkswagen-van ladies. Never trusted a man driving one, but there's something about the ladies. The kind of woman who would wear a babushka, bake her own bread, and have meaningful dialogues with her children. Laura Johnson fit that image.

I headed back for Mountain Falls Road and the Munsky farm. Dalton was sitting where I had left him forty-five minutes earlier. He smiled brightly as I pulled up in front of the farmhouse.

"Hi, Milt. Didn't let nobody in," he said, standing.

I got out of the car and walked up to the front door. "Ya done good, Dalton. Just sit on back down there and keep up the good work."

Dalton sat as I let myself in the front door. I called Mike at the station and told him to call Moulini's secretary and see if anyone had used their place that weekend and also told him of the description of the man and car Mrs. Johnson had seen, telling him to put an APB out on it. But Mike had news of his own.

"This may be connected, Milt. There's been a series of rape/strangulations going on in the area. Two in Tejas County—one three weeks ago and one in June; and one in Bulger over the weekend of the Fourth of July, and another back in April in Lauden. You know, that little place over Tabor Country? And, listen to this, all of 'em old ladies! Youngest one was sixty-nine. Sick somabitch!"

"Yeah, ain't they all?" I agreed. I thanked him for the information and got a promise that he'd move on what I'd given him right away.

Then I sat down and got out my book and called up David Perry's alibi for the weekend. He had told me he had been with a couple in Tulsa, a gallery owner and his wife who were going to display some of his work. They had used the weekend to go over the details of the exhibit, Perry had said. The gallery owner's wife, Kiersten Mays, confirmed Perry's story. I thanked her and hung up. I didn't have much to go on except Mrs. Johnson's man in the green Chevy. I had to hope that somebody else may have seen him. I left Mrs. Munsky's house to go down the hill to the Falls and start asking questions down there.

TWO

DURING THE LAST TEN YEARS or so of our marriage, the wife had been after me to lose some weight. That was why, after she left me, I got back at her by gaining ten more pounds. I say I'm six foot tall, but my doctor's records show me as five-eleven and a half. I'd been teetering on the brink of two hundred pounds for all the years of the wife's complaining, but now I've definitely teetered over that chubby precipice. I'm not bald. I have a receding hairline. One of these days it's gonna recede back to my shoulder blades, but it's still a receding hairline.

In two months, I'm going to be forty-eight years old. That's about as close to half a century as I want to get, but, of course, the alternative to reaching fifty is death, so I might change my mind. For my mid-forties (I consider late forties to be forty-nine and a half), I don't look or feel all that bad. My hair's still the same color it was in high school, kind of a sandy brown, what's left of it. No gray. From a standing position I may not be able to see if my shoelaces are tied, but two weeks ago I chased a fifteen-year-old suspected convenience-store robber for ten miles and caught him. And I wasn't even out of breath. Of course, I was in my squad car at the time.

I don't usually go on like this about my looks. It's something that doesn't generally bother me one way or the other. But after leaving Laura Johnson's house, the way I looked was on my mind because the way she looked was on my mind.

What was it about that lady? The turquoise eyes? The long lashes? The half-naked breast? None of those things really stood out. What did was the vision of her, all of her, lifting the baby with a laugh and carrying him to his playpen. She moved like an animal, a big cat, maybe. Graceful but unconscious of it. A natural rhythm to the sway of her hips.

All the way from Mrs. Munsky's house, past the Johnson place, and on down the steep hill to the swamps and the bottom of the Falls, I couldn't get her out of my mind. Only a woman as naturally beautiful as she was could be so unconscious of it. I kept telling myself that this was a married lady with three little kids and I'd best keep my mind out of the gutter. But it didn't help. It just kept sloshing around down there with the winos and the cigarette butts.

Like I said earlier, there are no more houses after the Johnsons' place, even at the base of the hill where Mountain Falls Road turns automatically into Falls Road. But at the base of the Falls themselves is a place called Falls End, a tourist camp with camping spots around the pool at the bottom of the Falls, an RV area, and cabins.

A couple of years ago, the people on Mountain Falls had gotten fed up with the tourists at the camp screeching their dirt bikes up and down the road, so, with the cooperation of the county, they had blocked off the two-mile stretch from the swamp up the hill to the other end of the Munsky place, where the hill descended again to Highway 5. The tourists could get to Falls End on Falls Road from another entrance off

Highway 5 and had no real reason for going up Mountain Falls Road except to gawk at the great view of the falls. The Mountain Falls Road people paid for half of the repair work on the road in exchange for signs on either end that said "Private Road—No Trespassing." So Mrs. Johnson having seen that green Chevy was significant. Whatever its occupant was doing on Mountain Falls Road, chances are it wasn't kosher.

I pulled into the entrance to Falls End and parked the squad car in front of the office and general store. Haywood Hunter owned and operated Falls End and had since its heyday back after World War II. Mountain Falls got fewer and fewer tourists over the years as natural beauty got outshone by the big amusement complexes like Six Flags down in Dallas.

On this Wednesday in early August, with the sun beating down hot enough to fry your brain, there were only two campsites occupied and three RVs parked in the RV area. I went into the coolness of the general store and saw Haywood sitting behind the counter, feet propped up on the counter like he owned the place, which he did, reading a *Playboy* magazine.

"Don't you know looking at that stuff's gonna make you go blind?" I said as I entered.

Haywood didn't take his eyes off the magazine. "Be more fun in Braille, anyway."

"You hear about old Mrs. Munsky?"

He put his magazine down at that and shook his head. "Don't that beat all? Nice old lady like that. What's this world coming to?"

I nodded in agreement. "Need to ask you some questions, you got the time, Haywood."

He stood up and offered me a beer. I declined, being on duty and all, but accepted a cold Coke. Haywood was a barrel-chested man in his late sixties. His once blond hair had just sorta faded instead of going gray and, bless him, he had all of it. The one thing you noticed right off about Haywood Hunter was his nose. Which could make Carl Malden's look like it's been bobbed. The man did have a honker on him and that's the God's truth.

He and his wife had bought this place on a GI loan back in 1947. She'd run off with a guy in a shiny Airstream in 1954, leaving Haywood with their two boys, then ages seven and five. Both boys had married and moved out of the area years ago, and as far as I knew, had rarely come back. Haywood spent his days picking up people's trash and selling them canned goods, his evenings calling bingo under the pavilion he'd built back in the fifties, and his nights in the little apartment of his back of the store doing whatever it is lonely old men do.

"So what's on your mind, Milt?" he asked, opening his own beer and settling back in his chair.

I pulled a stool up to the counter and sat down with my Coke. It was gone in about three swallows, it was that hot out there.

"Wonder if you seen a guy, early thirties, stringy blond hair, driving a green Chevy Impala, 'bout a seventy model? Torn-up black vinyl top?"

Haywood thought for a long moment, then shook his head. "Naw. Don't ring a bell. Ain't got nobody here at the camp fits that description. Used to turn that type away, anyway," he said with a sigh, "but nowadays, I take what I can get. Riffraff and all."

"You see anything on Monday out of sorts? Car you didn't recognize coming offa Mountain Falls Road? Strangers?"

"Naw. Don't mean much, though. 'Cept early in the morning when I pick up the trash cans, I stay inside here mostly. Too hot to do anything else."

"What'ja got here now? How many here that were here Monday?"

Haywood reached for his registration book. "Let's see. Got the Browns—Mama, Papa, and two little Browns. They pulled in here Friday noon in that Winnebago. The Montgomerys, in the fifth wheeler. Retired couple, been here since last Wednesday, leaving today."

I nodded my head and wrote fast in my little book.

"And I got three boys from Longbranch camping out by the Falls since Saturday morning. You know Davy Patterson? His boy and two others from the Longbranch Cougars. Only thing they're into is drinking beer and hoping I won't notice. Dumb kids; who they think picks up the goddamn trash?"

I laughed like I was supposed to.

"And a honeymooning couple camped other side of the Falls, but they didn't pull in till last night. And two schoolteachers from Sherman, Texas, in that rental Cherokee, been here since Sunday. And that's the lot."

"Mind if I go talk to some of your people? Maybe they saw something, being outside all day, that you didn't."

"Sure. Just don't get nobody mad and don't scare the bejesus out of the ladies, okay, Milt?"

I grabbed another Coke to fortify myself against the raging heat and wandered over toward the Falls where

I saw a small crowd down at the little beach area. What had to be the two schoolteachers and the three high school boys were playing volleyball on the beach. I didn't blame the boys. The ladies may have been schoolteachers, but I wouldn't have minded being in either of their classes. Both were in bikini tops and cutoff jeans, neither looked over thirty, and both could rival the centerfold Haywood had been studying. I wondered why he looked at the magazine when he could just come down here and look at the schoolteachers. Probably because it wasn't air-conditioned down here. When looking was all you could do, you might as well be comfortable.

I showed my badge and ID and the group, consisting of the whole camp with the exception of the honeymoon couple, gathered around me. I explained why I was there and asked if any of them had seen anyone fitting the description Mrs. Johnson had given me. No one had. Neither had anyone seen anything or anyone suspicious on that Monday. As my old daddy used to say, I was shit out of luck.

I used the phone in Haywood's office to call Dalton at Mrs. Munsky's house. The phone rang ten times before I hung up. I had forgotten to tell Dalton to answer the phone when it rang. My own fault.

I went back up the hill to Mountain Falls Road, wondering if I'd have to get out and push the squad car up it. The county cutbacks were getting bad. The engine of the squad car needed to be overhauled six months ago, but with the cutbacks, we were down to only one mechanic who handled all county vehicles, not just the sheriff's, and he was too busy taking care of the wrecked cars to deal with general maintenance.

I pulled into Mrs. Munsky's yard and hollered at Dalton through the open car window.

"Going on back to Longbranch now, Dalton. You just sit tight. And answer the phone when it rings, okay?"

"Sure, Milt. Nothing to it." I left him grinning and sitting on the front porch and headed down the other side of the hill to Highway 5.

It was eighteen miles from Mountain Falls Road to the county seat of Longbranch where the sheriff's office was located. The wife had used that as her main argument against moving to the crazy house on Mountain Falls Road. "You gonna commute thirty-six miles a day, Milton? When am I gonna see you, alternate Wednesdays?" That woman always did have a smart mouth on her.

I pulled my car into my own personal parking space. That little perk came with the fancy title. The Sheriff's Department was housed in its own building, which had been built back in the late seventies with proceeds from a special bond issue. Until then, we had been housed in a corner of the County Courthouse, along with the Longbranch Police Department. That had been very confusing for the good people of Longbranch. We handled county trouble, the police department city trouble, and never the twain shall meet, so to speak. But since our office was before the police department's office from the main doors of the courthouse, we got all the traffic. Missy Lauderback, our sixty-year-old clerk, had spent most of her time directing city people to the police department.

The new building (it'll be called that when we reach the year 2000) was long and low and made of cinder blocks. The bond issue hadn't been a big one. The front door where the citizenry came in faced a long counter where our new clerk (Missy retired five years years ago), Gladys Webster, held court. Gladys was a no-nonsense lady in her mid-forties with absolutely no sense of humor. If I were casting a movie with a character of a spinsterish librarian, I'd have picked Gladys Webster for the part. In reality, she was married and had three teenage boys. You'd think you'd have to have a sense of humor in a household like that.

Behind Gladys' counter was the deputy bullpen. We had five in all, six if you counted me; two for days, with me making the third, and three for nights. And also back in the bullpen was the computer terminal. We got that with a special bond issue last year. Now all we needed was a bond issue to pay the salary of someone to work the damn thing. If we had that someone now, we'd have probably already known about the other rape/strangulations in the area. As it stood, the information was probably in a flyer in somebody's in basket gathering dust.

To the right of the bullpen area were the interrogation rooms and holding cells, all of them empty right now. To the left was a hall that led to my office, the county coroner's office (although he did all his real work at the Country Hospital, he still had an office here), the day sergeant's office, and the sheriff's office. At the end of the hall was a door that led out to the parking lot that was to be used by sheriff's personnel only. That's the door I came in and the first door as I entered was the sheriff's office. I went in and reported on Mrs. Munsky's murder.

The sheriff of Prophesy County is an elected office. And Elberry Blankenship had been elected to that office every two years for the past twenty years. It was rare that someone had the nerve to run against him, but at least every ten years or so, somebody would. Why somebody'd spend the money to do it, I don't know. The sheriff never spent a dime on campaigning. He'd just spread the word he was running again as usual and everybody except maybe the mother of the guy running against him would vote for Elberry Blankenship. Including me. He was a good man.

He might look like Hollywood's version of a hick sheriff, but he wasn't. He was fifty-five years old, about five feet seven, and could stand to lose about thirty pounds. Or maybe forty. He always wore a uniform, the belt of which hung below his protruding belly. He was bald as an egg and wore an old felt cowboy hat whenever he left his office. And he had a pair of snakeskin cowboy boots, probably as old as he was, that I'd've given my right arm for.

But he was good. He knew his business. He'd been a deputy under the former sheriff, a mean, corrupt old man that he'd run against twice before the county had enough and voted Elberry in. I wasn't around then, but some of the old-timers who liked to come by and chew the fat told stories of the changes he made the day after his election. In essence, Elberry Blankenship brought the Prophesy County Sheriff's Department out of its post-Civil-War depression and into the present. In his twenty years as sheriff, he'd hired an Indian, a black, and a woman as deputies, events which the prophets of Prophesy declared each time would cost him his next election. It never did.

"You get an APB out on that green Chevy?" he asked me after I reported.

"Yes, sir, sure did."

"What's your next step?"

"Well, guess I'll go see if Mike got ahold of Moulini's secretary and see if anybody was at their place this weekend. Off chance, though. Then talk to the other agencies handling the similar cases, see if they have any suspects might match up to ours."

"Okay."

"Maybe check up on them three high school boys at the Falls?"

"What about this artist? What's his name? Perry? You only got the one confirmation about where he was?"

I'm not as stupid as I look. "Yeah, I'll look into that further. But I swear to God, Sheriff, leads are thinner than spaghetti."

"Better check up on the Johnson woman's husband while you're about it," he said.

Now I hadn't thought about that. I guess I didn't want to admit to myself that she had one.

I went into my office and checked my notes. Mrs. Johnson had told me her husband worked for Swensen's Farm Machinery as a salesman. I called their office, which was right outside of Longbranch, and talked to the receptionist. According to her records, Jerry Johnson had been in Bulger, county seat of Tabor County, on Monday, doing business as usual.

In thinking over the sheriff's suggestions, I wondered if I'd have to drive all the way to Tulsa to confirm David Perry's story. I hadn't been to Tulsa in about a year, but thinking of going there got me to thinking about El Troja, a Mexican-food restaurant there that served the best enchiladas I'd ever eaten. Thinking earlier about Laura Johnson, I'd decided maybe I should lose a few pounds. Now I figured that could wait until after my trip to Tulsa, if I got to make it.

I left my office and went to the bullpen to see Mike Neils. He was just hanging up the phone.

"That was Dalton. I was calling to see if you were still there. Why didn't you let me know you were back? I have the information you wanted from Mr. Moulini's secretary. Boy, this is the biggest case I've ever been on. I put the APB out on that guy in the green Chevy. Did you find out anything else? Maybe we should get search warrants, what'ja think? Or check with that old man at Falls End? Maybe we could..."

"Whoa, boy. Steady now." He finally took a breath. I almost expected his tongue to loll out. "Come on back to my office and give me the report from Moulini's secretary."

"Yeah, sure, Milt. Boy, this is something."

Once he was settled in my one visitor's chair, he told me Moulini's secretary's name was Wanda and her voice sounded like she had big tits. I wondered about that but let it go. The gist of the report was that Wanda wasn't sure if anyone had been up there that weekend or not. Someone had borrowed the key saying they might, but hadn't informed her that they were definitely going. She was going to call the person in question and find out and call Mike back.

Billy Moulini, who owned the mountain-cabin chateau on Mountain Falls Road, was a retired plumbing contractor from Oklahoma City who had made it in a big way. I understand the old boy was worth several million. Coral was his third wife and getting a little long in the tooth for Billy's tastes. I figured if Wanda the secretary did have big tits and was young enough, she might be number four for old Billy.

Now in his late sixties, he had been raised in Bishop, a little community here in Prophesy County near Longbranch, and had played ball for the Longbranch Cougars back in the thirties. He dropped out of high school, though, as I understand it, before his senior year (a success story most Prophesy County parents tried to keep from their teenage sons) and had gone on to the big city to make his fortune. And he did. He came back to Prophesy County with his first wife to build the mountain-cabin chateau and brought back each successive wife for a honeymoon. I'd met him at fund-raisers and other county functions. He was one of those back-slapping, jovial types who make you want to rip out their lives on the spot. But the sheriff said to tolerate him because he brought a lot of money into the county with his charitable contributions and such.

I realized Mike was talking. Talking and squirming in his chair like a little boy needing to pee. "Maybe I should go back out to my desk, Milt, case she calls."

I sighed. "Mike, they'll come get you if you get a phone call. But you go on back now anyway. I'm through with you." I flipped through the notes in my book and tore out a page. "These are the people staying out at Falls End. The ones not crossed off've been there since before the murder. Do some preliminary checking for me. Start with the three high school boys from here."

Mike stood and looked at the list I handed him. "Jimmy Patterson? I know him. My little brother's in his class. Milt, these boys . . ."

"I know, I know. Just do me the favor and check 'em out anyway, okay?"

"Sure, Milt," he sighed, "but gee—"

Gee? God, give me some grown-ups to work with!

Mike left my office and I got on the phone to Bill Williams, deputy sheriff of Tejas County.

"Hey, Bill," I said when the clerk finally got me through to him, "how you doing?"

"Hey yourself, Milton. Fine. You?"

"Fine."

"Hear you met up with our rapist out your way?"

"Yeah. Victim's a Mrs. Beatrice Munsky. Window of old Olan Munsky?"

"Oh, yeah. LeRoy's mama, right? He runs the garage on Highway 5 near Bishop?"

"That's the one."

"Shit. Damn shame. How's old LeRoy holding up?"

"Okay, I guess." I hadn't seen any of the family members; the sheriff had handled that part himself, thank God.

"Well, can't tell you much about the two we had here. Both old women living alone. One was dead at least a week before we found her. Jesus, that was something, let me tell you! An old maid living on her dead daddy's farm. Still be there if the mailman hadn't smelled her. The other one, our coroner said she'd been dead just a few hours when a neighbor found her.

Nobody saw nothing either time. Coroner said they'd been raped all right, but no semen in either of 'em. Either the guy's got more of a problem than the obvious one or he's wearing a rubber.''

''Kinda polite for a murderer, don't you think?''

''True, true. We dusted both places for prints but didn't find nothing. No tire marks in the driveway, and the second one—where we found the lady right off?—well, that was a dirt road and it'd been raining. So what we got is exactly zip.''

So I told him about the blond guy in the green Chevy.

''No shit! That's great! I'll put it on the horn here. Maybe we'll pick something up, never can tell.''

I thanked Bill, hung up, and dialed again. This time I called the hospital and asked to speak to the county coroner. The coroner, Dr. Jim Macher, was in his fifties and had taken on the job of county coroner eleven years before, balancing it with a private practice. After five years, he had given up the private practice and concentrated on working with the dead alone. He said it was quieter that way. You didn't have to listen to *them* complain about their hemorrhoids.

He was a fairly nice man, except for his macabre sense of humor. I didn't mind dealing with him when he was in his office here in the sheriff's department, but when he was at the morgue at the Country Hospital, he could get real disgusting real fast.

''Hey, Dr. Jim, it's Milt.''

''Hi, Milt. Guess you're calling about Mrs. Munsky, huh?''

''One quick question. You find any semen?''

"That's what I was about to tell you, boy, if you'd shut up long enough to listen. Nary a trace. But the lady'd been raped all right, bruises around the vaginal opening..."

"That's okay, Dr. Jim. Just wanted to know about the semen. Thanks."

That was the thing about Dr. Jim when he was at the hospital. Details. He loved to give you details. And I didn't want to hear them. I figured it was bad enough the way Mrs. Munsky died without having some stranger like me know all the indignity she'd suffered.

But the information he gave me fit what Bill Williams had said. It was the same guy, more than likely. And he was either having the same problem or was still being polite. Whichever.

THREE

THE WIFE'S LAWYER and my lawyer had decided the fair thing would be to sell our house, the one we bought when we didn't buy the house on Mountain Falls Road, and split the equity. She, of course, would get the furniture, the new car, and custody of the dog.

That was all just fine and dandy with me. I hated the house, mostly because it wasn't the house on Mountain Falls Road. It was a nice enough little three-bedroom, two-bath. Looked just like every other house on the block, up to and including the three bushes by the front steps. The furniture was all of the wife's choosing—like I said before, heavy French provincial. She let me have the old bedroom suite that was in what we called the guest room. This was the bed we'd started our marriage in. I had a sentimental attachment to the bed my beloved had lost her virginity on, but she didn't seem to care, if she remembered. So I got the old bed, old dresser, and old nightstand, plus my chair that had been relegated to the garage because it didn't go with the foofaraws.

The dog was one of those nervous miniature poodles, a dirty-white color they call champagne for some stupid reason. Her full name, on her papers (the damn dog had papers!) was Blessed Jeanne de Prophesy. Can you believe it? Guess whose idea that was? The wife called her Jeannie-poo for short. I called her that goddamn mutt. I always thought maybe we should've had kids, but they never came. I did everything right, as far as I knew how, but no kids. Maybe, what with the divorce and all, it was for the best.

After she moved out and her lawyer notified me that I had to vacate the house so we could sell it, I had to move. Longbranch isn't one of those towns with lots of singles' apartments and condos and such. Actually, there's only one apartment complex in the whole town and it's pretty bad. It's a government housing project for Indians coming to the city. That's what they call Longbranch, though it's really not big enough to be called a city.

So I had to find a place to live. The sheriff came through for me on that one. His mother's cousin, Eva Jean Horne, had just been widowed and was thinking of renting out the back of her house to supplement her husband's Social Security and small pension. So I went to see Mrs. Horne and we agreed that the arrangement might work. After a month of living in a dingy room at the Longbranch Inn, I moved into the back portion of Mrs. Horne's house.

She'd cut the place in half down the middle widthwise, and had a small kitchenette added. That gave me a sitting room, bedroom, bath, and kitchenette, all paneled in this god-awful plywood paneling stained an orangy brown. It was all I needed. I moved in with my chair, my bedroom suite, and a plant given to me as a house-warming gift by the staff of the Sheriff's Department.

So, around six o'clock on that Wednesday evening, I pulled into the driveway of my home and saw Mrs. Horne outside watering her prizewinning begonias. They were beauties, too, if you were into begonias. I'm not, particularly. Until I moved in with Mrs. Horne, I didn't know a begonia from a peony. But then I'm admittedly flower-stupid, and, according to the wife, flower-stingy.

"Hey, Miz Horne!" I greeted her as I got out of my personal car, a '55 Chevy four-door I've had since high school. Cherry condition. Original paint job. Original seats, covered in plastic to keep 'em original.

"Well, hey, yourself, Mr. Kovak. Fine evening!"

I walked up to her and watched silently as she watered the begonias. Finally, I said, "Miz Horne, you hear about Mrs. Munsky?"

She shook her head sadly. "Yes, dear Lord, I surely did." A tear fell down her cheek. "Such a nice woman. We were both in the ladies' auxiliary at the Baptist church. Been on the same committees. That woman'd never hurt a fly, know what I mean?"

"Yes, ma'am, I do. Senseless."

We stood in the early-evening sun and watched the water splash gently on the flowers. I cleared my throat. "Miz Horne, there's a maniac loose, ma'am. You need to be aware of that."

"You don't know yet who done it, huh?" She looked up at me, her curly gray hair, newly permed at Debbie's Cut and Curl, bright in the sun.

"No, ma'am. Not yet. But I'm gonna find the— creep. But meanwhile, Miz Horne, you don't let anybody in. For anything. No matter what time of the day. I'm talking about somebody delivering flowers, or with a car out of gas and needing to use the phone—anything. Even if you know 'em. You don't let 'em in unless you got somebody else in the house with you, preferably a man that's kin."

She nodded her head. "All right, Mr. Kovak. It's a right shame, though, when a woman can't even let in her neighbors without fearing for her life."

"Well, that's the God's truth, but just the same..."

"I won't let anybody in, Mr. Kovak. And if anybody does try messing with me, well, I got my Earl's shotgun right there in the house and I suppose I'll just have to blow 'em away. That's all right, isn't it?"

I smiled. "Yes, ma'am. That'll be just fine."

I left her watering her begonias and went to my part of the house for my first beer of the day. It was nice, that first beer every evening, especially nice when I didn't have the wife shooting daggers at me with her eyes for drinking it. But as the last of the contents of my first can slid down my throat, I thought about Laura Johnson. And decided to switch to light beer.

Before I left the station, I'd called the agencies where the other rape/strangulations had occurred, the police department in Bulger, and the sheriff's office in Tabor County that had jurisdiction over the little town of Lauden. The officer in charge of the case in Bulger gave me the same information as Bill Williams from Tejas County had. No semen, no prints, no nothing. Same in Lauden.

I'd talked to Sheriff Blankenship about following up on David Perry's alibi in Tulsa and he said going to Tulsa sounded like a good idea, but I'd have to take my own car and pay for my own gas, what with the county cutbacks and all. I agreed. I knew my '55 had a better chance of making it all the way to Tulsa than the department's two-year-old Plymouth.

I had some paperwork to finish up at the station, so I figured I'd get there early, do the work, and leave for

Tulsa no later than nine-thirty or so. It was at best a two-hour drive and I wanted to be there in time for lunch. My fantasy about El Troja's enchiladas was growing by leaps and bounds. So I was determined to get to bed early. I fixed myself a Lean Cuisine I had in the freezer, drank two more beers, and watched some TV, then crawled into the bed around ten o'clock.

At midnight, I was still staring at the ceiling and still thinking about Laura Johnson. The wife and I had been married for twenty-seven years. And I never messed around on her. I'd thought about it, fantasized about it, even planned it one time, but I'd never done it. When she walked out six months ago, I decided to do something about it and went to bed with Glenda Sue Robertson, the waitress at the Longbranch Inn's restaurant. Glenda Sue had been flirting with me off and on for the past ten years. So I took her up on it. Once. After twenty-seven years, I felt so goddamn guilty it was ridiculous. She was real nice about it, but I stopped eating at the Longbranch after that.

Laura Johnson was the first woman I'd met since the divorce that I really wanted. And I wasn't sure why. She was married. She was at least ten years younger than me. She had three little kids. But, Lord, did I want that woman! Sometime in the wee hours of the morning, I fell asleep. And dreamed about the wife. Which I figured wasn't fair at all.

Now, Tulsa's a pretty town. May not be LA, or New York, or Miami, but it's a pretty town. Lots of trees and old houses. Lots of class. I'd thought about moving there when I got out of the Air Force, but the wife, who I married immediately after my discharge, didn't want to be that far away from her mama, who lived in Bishop.

So we stayed in Prophesy County and I worked for her daddy at his lumber store for a few years, then sold cars at her cousin's used-car lot for a few more years before I got the job as a deputy with the Sheriff's Department. But I went to Tulsa as often as I could, and even if the county wasn't paying for this trip, it was nice to get to go on a weekday. If I played my cards right and submitted an expense voucher with all the *i*'s dotted and all the *t*'s crossed, maybe they'd reimburse me for the meal at El Troja. That is, if that was in the rule book this week.

The county cutbacks were caused by the oil glut, following so quickly on the heels of the oil shortage, which I still find a bit puzzling. Everybody who thinks about oil thinks about Texas, but here in Oklahoma we've always done a big business in oil. Texas just gets all the publicity. But we got hit just as bad as those fat cats in Houston and Midland/Odessa. But don't get me started on Texas or Texans. Don't get any Oklahoman started on that. Can't shut us up. Suppose you heard that if they gave the world an enema, they'd stick the end of the hose in Texas, and nobody'd notice? And I suppose you already know that there's a sign at the Oklahoma-Texas border that says, ''Texas This Way'' and everybody that can read turns around and heads back to Oklahoma?

I pulled into the parking lot of El Troja at five minutes to noon. Which gave me a head start on the lunch crowd. I found a good table in the No Smoking section and told the pretty little girl waiting on my table that I didn't need a menu. Just the enchilada special and a Carta Blanca. She smiled and went off for my basket of tostadas and dish of hot sauce.

The service at the El Troja was fairly good and I was only on my second basket of tostadas when my enchiladas came. Ambrosia. Food for the gods. I took off my jacket, managing to bunch it up beside me in the booth, where it covered my hip holster and .45. I was wearing a short-sleeved shirt, which is the best thing to wear when eating El Troja enchiladas. The grease ran down to my elbow and down my chin and I was in hog heaven. I finished off the enchiladas, rice and beans, belched into my napkin the way my mama taught me, and took my leave with a sigh.

I checked in at the Tulsa Police Station with a Detective Pruitt, told him my business in his town, and asked him if he might have anything on David Perry, or his alibis, Blocker or Kiersten Mays. All he had was three outstanding parking tickets on Blocker Mays, all at the address of his gallery, and a speeding ticket on Kiersten that was a week overdue in being paid. I thanked him and decided to try their home address first.

It was one of those houses that had been ultramodern in the 1950s, long and low, made out of redwood and white brick with lots of glass. No garage but a carport covered in some kind of creeping vine—like I told you, I'm not real good on flowers and such. There was a sixties vintage MG in the carport. I pulled up behind it, got out of the car and wiped my face with my handkerchief. It was hotter than hell and I was sweating like a pig but I couldn't take off my seersucker jacket because of the hip holster. The trials and tribulations of a peace officer, I swear to God.

I walked up the brick walkway to the front door. The whole walk was surrounded with vegetation of some sort or another. Tropical-looking stuff that I'm sure they had to cover with something in the wintertime. The front door was one of those ornate-looking things with lots of gewgaws behind a modern glass-and-screen storm door. I pushed the button next to the door about four times before I got the hint that nobody was coming. I walked back to my car and that's when I noticed the old lady next door. Just the kind I wanted. The kind whose husband died or was so boring he couldn't keep her interest. The kind whose interest was mostly in her neighbors.

She was standing on the front porch, arms crossing her skinny chest and staring at me like it was the polite thing to do. I smiled and walked up to her, deftly stepping over the small row flowers and such that bordered the two yards.

"Hello, ma'am? I was wondering if you might be able to help me out?"

She just stood there staring at me and the look on her face reminded me of a teacher I'd had in the fifth grade whose greatest pleasure in life had been inflicting pain.

"I was looking for Mr. or Mrs. Mays. Live next door to you here?"

She didn't move a muscle except the one controlling her left eyebrow. That raised about a quarter of an inch.

"Ma'am?"

"What do you want to know about *them*?"

"Well, would you know where they might be?"

"He's probably at that gallery."

She said the word "gallery" like some people might say "snake pit."

"And Mrs. Mays?"

She snorted. Actually snorted.

"Where would her type be on a day like this?" she said. "If she's not lazin' around that pool of hers out back, she's probably out buying something. Far as I know, those are the only two things she does."

I had gotten enough about how she felt about the Mayses to know how to play her. You learn these things when you have a job like mine. So I showed her my badge and ID.

"Drugs?" she asked. I swear to God, there was a sparkle in her eye when she asked that.

"I'm not at liberty to say, ma'am." That would keep her the queen of the gossip mills for a month. "Could you tell me, ma'am, if you saw any company over at the Mayses' house this weekend? Tall guy with a beard?"

She snorted again. "Didn't see *him*—Mr. Mays—all weekend. Not till yesterday. Or any other man. *She* was here, though. All weekend. Hanging around the pool of hers in the skimpiest bikini you ever saw. Just daring men to peek over the fence at her. She's a public nuisance as far as I'm concerned."

"But Mr. Mays wasn't at home at all?"

"Never saw him or that fancy car of his."

"And you didn't see a guy, tall, kinda skinny, beard, bushy hair, kinda long? You didn't see him either?"

"Like I said before, I didn't see nobody but her flauntin' herself."

I thanked her and got in my car, wondering who was lying—the old bat or David Perry and Kiersten Mays?

I drove to the address for the gallery. It was in one of those cutesy-poo shopping centers where you couldn't buy a damn thing you actually needed. All the stores were specialty shops: Say Cheese, a wine-and-cheese specialty store; Slummin', a boutique that specialized in nothing, apparently, except denim clothing, with a miniskirt in the window costing $190 that used less cloth than one leg of my jeans; JJ Marsh, a "men's" shop with lots of cutesy outback clothes that had to be dry-cleaned; Footloose, with lots of running shoes and running clothes if you didn't mind sweating in two hundred dollars' worth of duds; and Blocker Mays Gallery, the place I was looking for.

The center itself was all painted white brick and dark wood, with discreet little brass plaques announcing each establishment. I figured it wasn't doing too well, as there were at least three empty storefronts that I could see on the ground level. I didn't really care what was upstairs.

There was a three-legged woman sitting in the window of the gallery, staring glassy-eyed at me. She was made out of some sort of cloth and had orange hair that was made out of what looked like the end of an old-fashioned mop. She was dressed in what my mama used to call a housedress, one of those loose, ugly, small-print things that some old ladies still wear. I figured if this is what Blocker Mays considered art, he and I weren't going to see eye to eye. Give me a good old Norman Rockwell any old day.

Inside there were other treasures of the same magnitude as the three-legged lady, like a hanger—really, a plain wire closet hanger—with what looked like dry-cleaning bags tied to it. With a price tag of $3,500. I swear to God! There were paintings on the walls, mostly abstract, none of which looked like anything I'd seen in David Perry's living room. Perry's work had been charcoal and chalk, mostly pictures of people and other things I could actually recognize. Of course, I figured his exhibition hadn't started yet.

But mostly, there was just a bunch of weird sculpture-looking things. As far as I was concerned, the Blocker Mays Gallery wasn't even worth browsing through.

When I walked through the door, a little bell announced my arrival. I had time to figure out I wouldn't be taking out any government loans to buy any of this stuff before someone came out from a room at the back to greet me. The someone was a man, about forty-five, short, totally bald, not even a little fringe—you know, Kojak-bald—wearing a lightweight summer suit the price tag of which, I am sure, would make Slummin's price tags look like Goodwill stuff. His mouth smiled but his eyes didn't. I figured my seersucker suit told him I wasn't buying any of his "art."

"May I help you?" The tone said he figured I'd walked into the wrong place or I needed to use the bathroom.

"I'm looking for Blocker Mays," I said, holding out my badge and ID.

He took both and studied them, looked from the picture on the ID to my face, then back at the picture. It wasn't that good of a picture, I grant you, but it did bear some resemblance to me. Finally, he handed me back both and looked at me for a full thirty seconds before he said, "I'm Blocker Mays. What can I do for you?"

"I need to ask you a few questions about one of your artists, Mr. Mays. A David Perry?"

"Yes?"

"Could you tell me if you know where Mr. Perry was this past weekend? From, say, Friday until Wednesday?"

He smiled. I figured that smile cost more than my house, when I had a house. "Why, of course, officer. David was with my wife and me all weekend. He got to our home around three Friday afternoon and didn't leave until Wednesday morning."

Well, this was interesting. I mused for a moment, then asked, "And you were there, at your home, all that time?"

"Well, no, of course not. We were here at the gallery a great deal of the time, working out spacing for his exhibit, which will start next month. Mr. Perry is a very fine artist."

"Yeah. I've seen some of his work." I looked pointedly at the things hanging now in the gallery. "Different than what you have in here now."

Mays smiled again. I was afraid he was going to pat me on the head, the smile was so patronizing. "We do different theme exhibits. What we have here are some very daring examples of the more modern interpretation of life and its frailties."

I nodded my head. "So—you were home all weekend?"

"As I've said, officer. And Mr. Perry was our guest. I can't say he was out of my sight or my wife's the entire time he was here."

"You have any other home than the one on Dempler Drive?"

He stiffened. I wondered why. "Just a lake place we seldom ever go to."

"I see. So you and Mr. Perry and your wife spent the whole time from Friday to Wednesday at your home on Dempler Drive?"

He sighed. He really had better things to do, obviously, than put up with me. "I've already told you that, officer."

I smiled. "Actually, it's chief deputy, but never mind. Thank you for your time, Mr. Mays."

I left the gallery and went back to my car, which was now about 105 degrees, and wrote some stuff in my notebook. Mainly: Who's lying? The old lady next door (Mrs. Murdock her name was) or Perry and the Mayses? Why would the old lady lie? Why would the Mayses? Why would Perry? If Mrs. Mays was home and Mr. Mays and Perry weren't, where were they? And why? I decided to go back to Dempler Drive and see if Mrs. Mays was home yet.

Mrs. Murdock was looking out her window when I pulled up. The MG was still in the carport. As I got out of the car, Mrs. Murdock came to greet me.

"She's out back. Was all the time you were here earlier. I bet she says she didn't hear the bell, but let me tell you, I could hear it at my place! You just wait and see if I'm not right!" She turned abruptly and walked back into her house, probably so she could go

out the back door and hear what I said to Mrs. Mays.
God, I love old ladies!

There was a wrought-iron gate at the back of the
carport. I went through the carport and up to the gate.
Through there I could see the backyard, complete with
pool and blond. I knocked on the wooden side of the
gate and called out.

"Mrs. Mays?"

The blond sat up in the chaise where she was and
turned. Standing, I got the whole view and understood why the men in the neighborhood might spend
the better part of their days peeking through the fence.
As she came closer. I could see that she had to be at
least six feet one or two. A good bit taller than me in
her bare feet. And she was *well*-proportioned. She had
a waist so tiny she looked like she'd been squeezed in
the middle. The swell of hips was perfect and the
breasts were outstanding. Well-put-together lady all
around. Her face, when you finally got around to
looking at it, wasn't bad either. Square-cut with strong
features, it was quite striking. And the hair, lots and
lots of blond hair, fell well beyond the strap of her bikini top. I couldn't help thinking, though, that she
couldn't hold a candle to Laura Johnson.

I showed her my badge and ID. And she smiled.
Great smile. Had to cost as much as her husband's.

"Yes. We talked on the phone." I noticed a slight
accent I hadn't caught on the phone. I figured she had
to be Scandinavian.

"I just need to ask you a few more questions, Mrs.
Mays."

She opened the gate and ushered me in. "Certainly, Chief Deputy." Chief Deputy? Her husband

must've just called. When we walked to the poolside, I noticed a cordless phone on the table next to her chaise. She pointed to a chair near hers and I sat. It was one of those lawn chairs with the strips of plastic going only one way across the bottom. I've always hated that kind of chair. Your butt hangs out. Very undignified.

"You said on the phone that Mr. Perry was visiting here from Friday until Wednesday, is that correct?"

She smiled. "Yes, he was."

"How come none of the neighbors saw him?" I like dropping bombshells. Catch 'em off guard, see what develops.

Nothing developed. She just smiled. "I have no idea."

"Ma'am?"

"I have no idea why none of the neighbors saw him."

"Well, they didn't see the car either. Or your husband's car."

"That's certainly interesting. But I don't understand why."

This was getting me no place in a hurry. I stood up. "Well, thank you for your time, Mrs. Mays, and if you ever do figure out why nobody saw either man here over the weekend, you'll let me know?"

She stood up too so that I had to look up as I delivered the last part of my little speech. A humbling experience.

"Of course, Chief Deputy." She smiled again and walked me to the gate.

FOUR

IT WAS after five o'clock when I got back to the station. Gladys was gone for the day; we only kept a clerk on from eight to five. After hours, a night deputy took over. The sheriff and I take turns being on call. Most of the time, it worked out just fine.

Jasmine Bodine was on duty tonight. Jasmine was our one woman deputy. Somehow, I always figured her parents should've named her Martha. The name they gave her and the genes they gave her just didn't match. She was on the scrawny side except for this big butt she had, making her look kinda like an avocado. Jasmine wasn't a real happy type either. Maybe because she was married to Lester Bodine. If I'd been a woman and I was married to Lester Bodine, I wouldn't be happy either.

I said hi and she looked at me for a long, sad minute and then said, "Hi," and turned and walked to her desk and sat down and looked sadly off into space. Her problem was that she knew what Lester was doing while she was working nights. She knew it, I knew it, and just about everybody in Longbranch knew it too. Especially the women.

The sheriff was still in his office. It was usually close to dinnertime before he headed home. I knocked on his door and went in to report.

After I'd given him the details of my day in Tulsa, excluding the enchiladas, I said, "It's strange. But I don't see where it's connected to Mrs. Munsky's murder.''

"You don't?" he asked, which meant, of course, that he did.

"Well—no, not exactly."

"Where were they? Blocker Mays and David Perry? And what were they doing?"

I didn't open my mouth and gape. I take great pride in that. "You mean—you think—*both* of them?"

"I'm not saying I think that, Milton, I'm saying it's a possibility. One you need to follow up on." With that, he looked down at some papers in his hand. I was dismissed and knew it.

Mike Neils was still there. I walked out to the deputies' bullpen and asked, "What time is somebody relieving Dalton up at Mrs. Munsky's?"

Mike looked up at me. "Sheriff called off the watch. Said there wasn't much need of it. Lab's pulled everything they're gonna pull outta there already. He's got Dalton out at Bishop. There was a robbery at the Food Land last night. Nine cases of canned peaches stolen."

"Looks like we got us a crime wave on our hands." I said this kind of under my breath, being a little put out that the sheriff had removed Dalton without telling me. Of course, I'd been in Tulsa, but just the same...

"What was that, Milt?" Mike asked.

"Nothing. Hear anything from Wanda Big Tits?"

Mike giggled. "I swear she ain't Indian!" He pulled out his notebook where he kept the most audacious notes you ever saw in your life. You fart around Mike and it'll wind up in that notebook. "Yeah, she called.

Seems like there was somebody up there this weekend after all. The guy just forgot to tell Wanda he was gonna go. Guy's name is Marshall—Stephen P. Lives in Oklahoma City—'' Mike read the address. "Came up here by himself, he says. I talked to him. Figured you'd want me to do that." I didn't. Today was the day to have my authority usurped, it looked like. "Says he didn't see or hear nothing all the time he was here. Says he left Sunday around four o'clock. So I guess that puts him in the clear."

"Oh, yeah? Who else says he left Sunday at four? You call up a guy on the phone and believe every goddamn word he says?" I didn't feel real good about that, but I was pissed.

"Gee, Milt. I see what you mean." The kid was so crestfallen I wanted to cry.

I got up and patted him on the shoulder. He looked up at me with such adoration I was afraid one of his hind legs would start beating the floor. "It's okay, Mike. Gotta take what you get at face value. But don't let go of it. Get confirmation. Tell me about the guy. Background."

I sat down at one of the empty deputy desks and let him read to me from his notes. "Wanda says the guy, Mr. Marshall, runs a plumbing-supply business. Big buddy of Mr. Moulini's. He says he got up to the mountain about seven P.M. Friday night and left around four Sunday. He says he didn't see nobody or hear nothing the whole time he was there. Says he went by himself because he needed some time off from work."

I mused aloud. "Hmm. A man needs time off from work, he usually goes hunting or fishing with some of the guys. Or if he's got a family, he stays home and cleans the gutters. Or goes on an outing with the wife and kiddees. Holing up in a cabin for two days all alone's not exactly natural."

"Gee, Milt, you've got a point there." This kid could get on your nerves in a hurry.

"Give me the number of this guy. Think I'll give him a try myself."

I didn't feel real good about that. Mike didn't either.

I took the number and went back to my office and dialed the Oklahoma City number. A woman answered the phone.

"Mr. Marshall, please?"

"May I say who's calling?"

"Chief Deputy Milton Kovak of the Prophesy County Sheriff's Department."

She left the phone and about thirty seconds later it was picked up.

"Yeah?"

"Mr. Marshall, this is—"

"Yeah. What do you want?"

"I wanted to ask you a few questions about your weekend here in Prophesy County, Mr. Marshall."

"I already told that punk that called before. I didn't see nothing, I didn't hear nothing. I don't know nothing."

And he hung up. Well, I have this theory about rude people. I figure they have something to hide. And I also figured my car could make it to Oklahoma City. Unfortunately, I also figured it would only be right to take Mike with me. That was gonna be a whole hell of a lot of fun.

That night was a lot like the night before. I drank the same number of beers with the same guilt thinking they should be lights, and spent the same amount of time thinking about Laura Johnson. And trying to come up with a reason to get me back to her end of Mountain Falls Road.

The next day, Friday, I got the reason. It was in the form of Mr. Stephen P. Marshall, owner and proprietor of the Marshall Plumbing Supply Company in Oklahoma City.

The trip to Oklahoma City had been about as much fun as I'd expected. Mike talked nonstop the whole way. He told me about his girl dumping him two weeks before and how maybe he might try to see Wanda Big Tits while he was there and just check her out, as they got on so well on the phone. He also told me about his mother, his father, his brother, his Aunt Lois who lived in Milwaukee, and I'm pretty sure a couple of hundred other people. I wondered about telling Mike how boring he was before he did this with someone whose sense of humor wasn't as acute as mine, and who might end up shooting Mike just to shut him up. But I didn't.

When we finally got to Oklahoma City and weaved our way through the traffic to Marshall's Plumbing Supply, we found a surprise. Mike and I walked though the doors and there in front of us was this blond guy of medium height with long, stringy-looking hair. Older than Laura's description, closer to forty than to thirty, but with sunglasses on, he could pass.

I asked him what kind of car he drove. He claimed it was an '83 Lincoln Town Car, silver. I figured the best thing to do was get old Stephen P. and Laura together and see what developed. If this was the guy in the green Chevy, with a legitimate reason for being on the mountain, everything could be kosher. Except, of course, that he claimed to have left on Sunday.

If anything, Stephen P. was even ruder face to face than on the phone. If he wasn't our rapist/murderer, I'd've gladly locked him up for being nothing more than an asshole.

"I told you people and I told you people I didn't see nothing, I didn't hear nothing, and I don't know nothing!" He said this as we were drawing out our badges and IDs. The man didn't beat around the bush. He just came right up and ripped the bush out of the ground and stepped on it.

"Mr. Marshall, we need your cooperation on this matter, if you don't mind," I said. I didn't want to be polite. I wanted to hit him in the nose. The guy got on my nerves real bad.

"Yeah, well, I do mind. I'm running a business here and I don't need any hick cops pestering me."

I resented that. Mike resented that. I figured I was going to bust this guy for something.

I decided to get real officious. I can do that real good. "Mr. Marshall, a man fitting your description was seen at the scene of the crime. You can either come back voluntarily to Longbranch for a lineup, or we can arrest you here on the spot as a potential suspect and haul you back to Longbranch. Your choice."

Now I didn't look at Mike before, during, or after I said that. As it wasn't strictly the truth and Mike more than likely would have his mouth hanging open. I didn't want to draw Stephen P.'s attention to that. The man fitting his description, of course, hadn't been seen at the scene of the crime, just near it, and I could no more haul this guy's butt to Longbranch than I could fly but I've always considered myself a damn decent poker player.

It was touch and go there for a minute. He blustered. He threatened calling his lawyer. And if he'd actually had one, he probably would have. And that would have been the ball game. But I figured a guy like this with a business no bigger than his probably didn't have a lawyer on retainer. I figured right. After all the blustering, threatening, and name calling, he finally agreed to come back to Longbranch. Mike would drive Stephen P's car with him in it and I would follow, stopping off on Mountain Falls Road to pick up the witness.

Now, to say I was excited as I drove back to Prophesy County would not be too great an exaggeration. For one thing, it was just plain exciting to drive back by myself without Mike's running monologue. But it was more than that; I just wasn't sure if I was excited the most about a possible suspect or about seeing Laura Johnson again.

It was after three o'clock when I pulled off Highway 5 up Mountain Falls Road. I passed by Mrs. Munsky's farmhouse, looking deserted and forlorn in the stifling heat, and David Perry's house, reminding myself he and I still had some unfinished business if Stephen P. didn't work out. I pulled into the drive leading to the crazy house of the Johnsons and stopped in front of the corral.

Laura was there, leaning against the fence with the baby sitting atop it, watching the two older kids working a horse and pony. She had one hand on the boy's diaper, holding him steady, and the other hand on her hip. She was wearing a baggy denim sleeveless dress. To me, she looked like Princess Di ready for a ball. She turned when she heard my car coming down the drive and was watching me as I got out of the car. She smiled and I stumbled on a rock in the road. Milton Kovak, sophisticate.

She pulled the baby off the fence and walked toward me.

"Hi, Chief Deputy." Did I mention what a great voice she had? Throaty, deep, but bell-clear. Did I mention that everything about this lady was choice? Real choice?

"Afternoon, Mrs. Johnson."

"Laura."

"Pardon?"

She extended her hand and I took it. The nails were still bitten to the quick, and they were still work-worn, but the touch was cool, the grasp firm, and the feel somewhat akin to an hour's foreplay with a normal woman.

Her smile deepened, making the dimple in her left cheek pucker up. "My name. Laura?"

"Oh. Milt." We shook and I let go of her hand a little quick. If I hadn't, it could have got embarrassing.

"Mrs. Johnson—Laura—I think maybe we have somebody we want you to look at. I hate to ask you, but I need you to come to Longbranch and see if you can pick this guy out of a lineup."

The smile vanished and in its place was a frown. She looked good that way, too. She'd've looked good bald, with no teeth, and wearing a tow sack.

"Problem, Milt." She nodded her head toward the VW van still parked where I'd last seen it. "I tried to go to the store this morning and found out the VW's on the fritz."

"Oh, no problem. I'll drive you to Longbranch and bring you back."

She smiled. "Great! Just there, though. I can get a ride back with my husband."

She had to say that. She just had to say that.

She turned to the kids and told them to water and brush the horses quickly and wash their hands and faces.

"While they're doing that, and I'm diapering this one," she said, "how'd you like to come in the house for a glass of iced tea?"

I followed her into the house and back to the kitchen. The kitchen table was built like a picnic table, with benches instead of chairs, out of pine. The refrigerator was covered with juvenile artwork: a purple-and-orange butterfly, a picture of Jesus with green hair, and the like. There were dishes drying in the drainboard and plants hanging everywhere.

She got a glass out of the drainboard and an ice tray out of the freezer and proceeded to pop out the ice, fill the glass with ice, refill the ice tray, place it back in the freezer; then she opened the refrigerator to take out the pitcher of tea, pour the tea in the glass—all with the baby hanging on one lovely hip. I swear to God, women kill me.

She handed me the glass and led me into the living room, indicating the chair for me to sit in. I sat while she deftly changed the baby.

"I know, I know," she said with a laugh. "He should be potty-trained by now. But he's my last and I guess I'm trying to keep him a baby as long as possible." She finished the job and set Adam down on the floor, pulling up his little plastic pants and shorts. Hell, what did I know about potty-training kids? He looked natural in the diaper to me, just like a baby should.

He scampered off to a pull toy by the front window and started playing with it, making the clackety-clack sound with it like they do.

"Three's the limit, huh?" I said by way of conversation.

The smile left again and the frown appeared. "No, actually, I planned on half a dozen—I'm slightly crazy. But—I lost a baby between Rebecca and Adam—had a hard time with Adam and had to have an operation..." She laughed. "I'm sorry. You don't want to hear this."

The front door banged opened and the two older children charged into the living room. "Where we going, Mama?" the boy asked.

Laura introduced me. The boy, Trent, was seven and going into the second grade. He had dark curly hair and big brown eyes. His face was serious. The girl, Rebecca, was five, and excited about starting kindergarten in the fall. She was a miniature of her mother, right down to the turquoise eyes and the dimple in the left cheek. She was going to be a real killer.

Laura said, "Remember me telling you about what happened to Mrs. Munsky?"

The children nodded their heads. "And remember me telling you that I may have seen a man who might know something about it?"

Again, the little heads went up and down. "Well, Chief Deputy Kovak thinks he may have found the man. He wants me to go to the Sheriff's Department with him and see."

"Can we go too? Can we?" Trent's eyes were big as saucers at the excitement of it all.

"Can we see the jail? And some bad guys? And handcuffs and guns?" This was the little girl.

I smiled at her. It was an easy thing to do. "Well, honey," I said, "we don't have any bad guys right now, but you can sure see the jail where we'll put 'em if we find any."

"All right!" Trent said and he and his sister did a high-five.

"Go wash your faces and hands and let's go. We don't want to keep the chief deputy waiting," their mother said.

She and I went out to the van with Adam while the older two washed up. She removed the baby seat from the backseat of the van and took it to my car and hooked it to the backseat. The kids came running and hollering out the front door as Laura finished buckling the baby in. She went back to lock up the house while I got the older kids buckled up. I'd had seat belts put in the '55 a couple of years ago when all the hoo-ha started about buckling-up. I figured as a public servant it was a good example. Every once in a while, I even wear one.

We drove the eighteen miles in what felt like record time. All the horror stories I'd heard about taking trips with children I figured just weren't true. We had a great time. We played I Spy, 20 Questions, the License Tag Game, and a new one for me called I'm Going to the Moon and I'm Taking..., which I lost. Adam gurgled and talked and giggled and hit the plastic bar of his car seat with his plastic set of keys and the big kids asked questions about being a deputy which I obliged by answering. We had a great time. Laura smiled a lot. I was beginning to realize I liked this lady. Above and beyond the obvious lust.

I pulled up to the front of the new building and led them in. Gladys was more than happy to take the baby, and Dalton, who was back from not solving his stolen-peaches case, was tickled pink to take the bigger kids on a tour of the jail.

We don't have an actual lineup room like they have in big-city police departments. What we do is, we put our suspects and a couple of good citizens in one of the interrogation rooms and take the witness to an adjoining room with a two-way mirror. Works for us.

Mike had everything set up when we got there. Besides Stephen P., sitting in the room were Alton Smith, a night deputy, Tobe Lydecker, a druggist, and Jasper Amberdash, a used-car salesman who worked right down the road from the new building. Alton, Tobe, and Jasper were all blonds.

I had Laura sit down in one of the black plastic-and-chrome chairs and we looked through the two-way mirror at the suspects. She frowned and studied each man in turn. She didn't even hesitate at Stephen P. Finally, she shook her head.

"I'm sorry, Milt," she said. "The man I saw just isn't there."

It was looking more and more like the man in the green Chevy that Laura had seen was probably our killer. But, unfortunately, the killer wasn't Stephen P. I was a little disappointed.

I got up and went to the other room, telling Mike he could let the lineup, all except Stephen P., go. I wanted to talk to old Stephen P. again, if for nothing other than to get on his nerves.

I thanked Laura for her trouble and she and I gathered up her children and I drove them to Swensen's Farm Machinery on the outskirts of town and dropped them off. She and the kids smiled and waved good-bye as I drove off, and for some reason I felt a little sad.

Stephen P. and Mike were waiting for me in the interrogation room. Mike was nervous and Stephen P. was pissed.

"How much longer you gonna keep me here, Kovak?"

I smiled. "Long as it takes, Mr. Marshall." I sat down across from him at the table. "Now, you gonna be a good boy and tell me why it was you were here in my county over the weekend?"

"I told you, work was getting to me! I just needed some time off by myself."

I harassed him a little longer, just enough to make me feel good and not enough for a lawsuit, and let him go. I couldn't help grinning at the thought of how

much gas that Lincoln Town Car would burn between here and Oklahoma City.

After he'd gone, I told Mike to get a hold of Wanda
Big Tits and get a key to the Moulini place. I wanted
a look around.

"We already got a key, Milt. Mr. Moulini left it here
a while back, in case there was any trouble out that
way."

I got the key and went on home, figuring I'd get
back up to Mountain Falls Road in the morning. I
wanted to have a look at that mountain-cabin chateau and have my little chat with David Perry. I also
thought, being so close, it might be nice to drop in on
Laura and the kids, but then I remembered tomorrow
was Saturday. Husbands, such as they are, are usually home on Saturdays. So much for that idea.

FIVE

As I WALKED in the door of my half of Mrs. Horne's house, the phone was ringing. I got a not-so-light beer out of the fridge (I still hadn't been to the store to stock up on my dietetic food and drink), popped the top and picked up the phone in one smooth movement. Laura Johnson had nothing on me. I said, "Hello," took a swig, and immediately felt guilty. It was the wife.

"Milton?" I could tell by her voice she had heard me swallow.

"Hey."

"I just thought you'd want to know Uncle Fred's in the hospital."

Uncle Fred was the only one of her relatives I could tolerate. I actually liked him.

"What's the matter?"

"We think maybe it was a stroke. I'm home now with Mother. She's taking it real hard." That was news?—the wife's mother took an ingrown toenail hard.

"What do the doctors say?"

"They're still with him. No word yet. Aunt Merle's there at the hospital. And the boys." The boys were forty-two and thirty-nine and dumb as posts. One owned a used-car dealership and the other was the Bishop Junior High School basketball coach. The wife's cousins. I had worked for Jesse selling cars before I'd gone with the Sheriff's Department, and he and I had gotten on about as well as a cobra and a mongoose. I just never was sure which one of us was the snake. Though I always bet on him.

"I'm really sorry to hear that, honey." Old habits die hard.

"Well, I just thought you'd want to know, that's all."

"What hospital's he in?"

"Longbranch Memorial. Room three-oh-two."

"Well, I'll try to get by."

"You don't have to do that. I just thought you'd want to know." Jesus, that woman could throw guilt like an Olympic discus gold-medal winner.

"No, I wanna go. I like Uncle Fred."

"Well, at least there's somebody in my family you like." Here we go again.

"I gotta go, honey. Thanks for calling."

"Milton?"

"Yeah?"

"The divorce is gonna be final as of Monday."

"Oh."

"Just thought you'd want to know."

"Well . . ."

"Good-bye, Milton."

"Yeah." But I said that to a dead line.

I drank two more beers and looked in the fridge. There was half a can of Vienna sausages and some green cheese. I changed into some grubbies and went out to Highway 5 to Rosalee's Mexican Restaurant. It sure as hell wasn't El Troja but the food was edible. I had two more Carta Blancas there and decided I sure could use getting laid.

In between thinking about Laura Johnson, Glenda Sue Robertson came to mind. I thought seriously about dropping by the Longbranch Inn around ten, when she got off, but then thought she'd probably say no after the way I'd behaved. And even if she said yes, I didn't feel very good about it. I might be a lot of things, but I've never been a user to my knowledge. And I knew I'd just be using Glenda Sue—closing my eyes and pretending she was Laura Johnson. Course, how was I to know whether or not, when we'd been together before, she hadn't closed her eyes and pretended I was Robert Redford? Which I'd've done if I'd been her.

I'd known Glenda Sue all my life, I guess. At least since first grade. In high school, she'd gone with one of my best friends, Lindsey Robertson, who we called Lin unless you wanted to get hit, which he was good at. She'd been Glenda Sue Davies then. She and Lin got married right out of high school and had a little girl about six months later. And that's when the trouble had started. Lin had never been real big on responsibility.

I didn't know about their troubles until I joined the Sheriff's Department and then I got to get in on 'em just like all the other deputies. Lin took to drink like some men take to sex. He liked it a lot. And when he was drinking, everything would be just fine, unless somebody said something he didn't like. Of course, saying hello to Lin could be something he didn't like. And it all went on Glenda Sue.

By the time I joined the force, their little girl was ten. Her name was Melissa and she was pretty and blond like her mama. And she'd be the one to call it in when her daddy got drunk and started hitting her mama. I never was sure why Glenda Sue stayed with him. You hear a lot about security, but any security Glenda Sue had she made herself. Lin never worked a lick in his life. Any money they had came from Glenda Sue's waitressing.

But she put up with it, and by the age of thirty, she looked almost fifty. There was a permanent scar on her neck from when he'd got her with a broken beer bottle, and her right arm never did work just right after he broke it that time. But then Lin made a fatal mistake. He messed with Melissa. And Glenda Sue damn near beat his brains out with a two-by-four. I guess, enough's enough. Somewhere within all of us is this mean little puppy that'll rise up when things pass that limit. And Glenda Sue's limit got passed.

After Lin got out of the hospital, he tried to go home to the trailer but Glenda Sue met him with his own shotgun and he ended up with seven pellets of birdshot in his butt. For about three weeks, he just kept on trying to go home and he just kept on going back to the hospital to have the birdshot removed from different parts of his anatomy. I finally had Glenda Sue come into the station and have a peace bond put on him so we could legally keep him away from her. She didn't really want to do it. I think her real goal at that point was to kill him, but I convinced her Melissa didn't need a dead daddy and a prison-bound mama.

So once we had the peace bond on him, we just kept hauling his ass to jail. After about a year of birdshot up the ass and jail time, Lin got the idea to leave town. I saw him about eight years ago in Lawton. He'd been born again. Said he hadn't had a drop of drink in a year and was married to a real nice little girl that he wouldn't hurt for the world. He asked if maybe he could see his daughter.

At that time, Melissa was up in Norman going to the college, but I didn't tell him that. I told him he'd have to talk to Glenda Sue. Far as I know, he never did. I guess maybe the memory of all that birdshot in the butt kept him away. I don't know. All I know is, Glenda Sue Robertson was a fine lady and I'd best not try using her or anybody else.

I went on home and watched the "Late Show" out of Tulsa (which I can pick up with my giant antenna I bought to tune in the Cowboy games. Which is the only good thing ever to come out of Texas—the Cowboys. 'Cept maybe Willie Nelson. I like Willie Nelson). It was the Friday-night horror show, one of those low-budget English vampire movies with Peter Cushing. I fell asleep in front of the TV with my seventh or eighth or twenty-second beer in my hand.

The next morning I woke up with a crick in my neck, a mouthful of worms, and a wet crotch. The beer had spilled sometime during the night. I stood under the shower for a year or two and brushed all the enamel off my teeth, got dressed, and headed to the Longbranch Memorial Hospital.

It was after nine when I got there and they were allowing visitors. Uncle Fred was in a semi-private room with an old man who looked like he'd died in 1947.

Aunt Merle was sitting by Uncle Fred's bed, knitting in hand, scolding him, as usual. "A man of your age climbing around on a roof like that! What were you thinking of, Fred Mager? You think you're twenty years old or something? You think you're invincible like Superman or something? Oh, hello, Milt.''

She said "Hello, Milt" in the same way some people might say "There's caca on the floor."

Uncle Fred, though, smiled when he turned his head toward me. I thought he looked pretty good for a man of seventy, stroke or no stroke.

"It wasn't a stroke," Aunt Merle said in that way she has of answering questions before they're asked. "Heat. Man lived in Oklahoma all his born days, you'd think he'd know better than to crawl around on the roof in the midday sun in August, for crying out loud."

"How you doing, Uncle Fred?" I asked.

He smiled. "Oh, okay . . .''

Aunt Merle cut in as usual. I doubt Uncle Fred ever finished a sentence in his life. "As well as can be expected under the circumstances, Milton. And how are you?"

It was kind of a dare to say I was doing fine.

"'Bout the same, Aunt Merle.'' I wasn't sure of the etiquette of divorce. Are you still supposed to address your wife's relatives like that? Or as of Monday, would they revert to Mr. and Mrs. Mager? Best to go to the library and check out Emily Post.

"Your wife and mother-in-law were here yesterday." That was supposed to mean something, the way she said that, but I wasn't sure what.

"Yes, ma'am. She called me at home last night and told me about Uncle Fred. Thought I'd come by and say 'hidy.' ''

"Well, that was mighty nice of you, boy," Uncle Fred managed to get in.

"You still working for that sheriff?" Aunt Merle asked. With the exception of the competition's mother, I figured Aunt Merle was the only one in the county who ever voted against Elberry Blankenship. And mainly because I worked for him. She didn't take kindly to me quitting her son.

"Yes, ma'am. Matter of fact, I'm supposed to be working right now. I'm in the middle of a case..."

"Humph! I heard about that Mrs. Munsky person. You doing anything about that?"

"Yes, ma'am."

"It's getting so a lady isn't safe in her own home, Milton. You better do something about that!"

"Yes, ma'am..."

"I mean, when you got a regular psycho running loose in Prophesy County I figure it's time to get a new sheriff that can do something about it. Bring in a whole new batch of deputies, too!"

"Well, Aunt Merle..."

"That's all I got to say on the subject, Milton Kovak."

"Yes, ma'am. Well, Uncle Fred—" He reached out a hand to me and I took it, noticing for the first time ever how old and wrinkled that hand was. "You get better real soon, ya hear?"

"Will do it, boy. You take care."

Aunt Merle added, "And you best stop drinking, boy. Just 'cause your wife walked out on you is no reason to turn into a bum. You smell like a brewery."

I thanked her and left.

I drove out of Longbranch on Highway 5 to Mountain Falls Road and pulled into David Perry's driveway. When I turned the car's engine off and got out I could hear the sound of metal on metal coming from a slight distance away. From farther down the road. I figured it was Mr. Johnson, working on the VW van. I fantasized a little about the kids being in the corral working the horses, Laura in the kitchen baking bread, with Adam on the floor beside her with a pot and a spoon. It made me sad.

I walked up **and knocked** on David Perry's front door.

"What?" It was the kind of "what" you hear after somebody's been disturbed by three phone calls in half an hour and somebody coming to the door trying to sell a carpet-cleaning service for his hardwood floors.

Perry came to the screen door and saw me and smiled. "Sorry, Milt. I'm trying to work and the phone's been ringing off the hook." What'd I tell you?

"Mind if I come in a minute, Mr. Perry? Got a few questions."

"Name's David, but come on in."

I followed him into the living room and sat down on the afghan-covered easy chair. There was a spring loose that tried to move up the crack of my ass. I had to wiggle around to get it placed a little better. Perry sat down on the couch, put his arm across the back and smiled.

Nice fella, I thought, if he didn't lie so goddamn much.

"Mr. Perry..."

"David."

"Yeah. We got a problem, David."

"What's that, Milt?"

"I can't find anybody that places you at the Mayses' house when you said you were there."

"What? Surely Blocker and Kiersten told you—"

"They say you were there, but the neighbors say you weren't. They, the neighbors, also say Mr. Mays wasn't there from Friday until Wednesday."

Perry grinned. "By neighbors, Milt, you wouldn't happen to mean that old biddy that lives next door, would you? Murdock, I think her name is?"

"I interviewed some of the neighbors, yes."

He kept grinning. An innocent grin. "Well, if you're basing any of your thinking on anything that old bitch told you, Milt, I'd think again. That lady has been after Blocker and Kiersten since they moved in four years ago. You wouldn't believe some of the things she's done! She's called and had their gas cut off. Saying they've moved! I swear! Once Blocker locked himself out of the house and was trying to get in through a window and she called the cops and told them someone was trying to break in. And this was after Blocker said hello to her and told her what he was doing! Just talk to the Tulsa police, they'll tell you! That old bitch is a real nuisance."

Police work can be a humbling experience.

"She's turned Kiersten in twice for indecent exposure because she wears a bikini in her own private pool! Of course, with a body like Kiersten's, she looks indecent in a winter coat!"

He laughed. I knew I should have talked to more than one neighbor. I was beginning to feel a little foolish. But I'd call Detective Pruitt when I got back to the station and verify that Mrs. Murdock had a nuisance rap sheet on her. No more taking anybody's word for anything, just like I told Mike.

I stood up. "Well, David, thanks for talking with me. I'll be in touch."

He walked me to the door. "Milt, you gotta watch those old ladies, you know?" He laughed me all the way to my car.

I pulled out of David Perry's driveway and went the eighth of a mile to Billy Moulini's cabin's drive. The cabin was tucked way back in the trees, but not as far back as the Johnsons' place and its view wasn't as spectacular. But the house was. It was a huge log cabin, two-story. I stopped my car and got out and, using the department's key, opened the door and went in.

I walked through the house getting the lay. The place was decorated in macho. Heavy dark furniture, lots of dead animals on the walls staring glassy-eyed at you as you walked along. Every room looked like that except what I took to be the master bedroom. This was obviously the room the wives got to decorate. I figured wife number three, Coral, had the same kind of taste as my wife, except with a bigger pocketbook behind it. The room was all foofaraws and gewgaws, lace and ruffles. Imagining burly Billy Moulini humping in that ruffly bed got a laugh out of me for sure.

I went back down to the living room and tried to find some trace of Stephen P.'s weekend occupation of the house. I found it in the trash can by the big rolltop desk. Lots of crumpled-up pieces of paper. I pulled them out of the trash and straightened them out. They were typed papers. And a not very good typist had done them. Lots of strikeovers and misspellings. And the more I read the more I wanted to burst our laughing or burst into tears. I wasn't sure which.

Page 42: "She tried to pull away but his lordship's grip was too tight. He pulled her roughly toward him."

Page 43. "She felt heat in her loins as she had never before felt. Her breasts hardened under his lips and she let out a soft moan that grew in intensity."

I swear to God!

Page 44: "He stood looking down at her, his hair tossled and hanging in his face. Her simple peasant dress was torn, exposing her fine large breasts and the softness of her thighs. He said, 'Now you will be mine forever,' and exposed his manhood to her."

I swear to God!

I began to admit to myself that maybe the only thing Stephen P. was guilty of was bad writing. I crammed the papers into my pocket to take back to the station. I had every intention in the world of sharing my new-found bounty.

I pulled out of the Moulinis' drive and headed up Mountain Falls Road, past the Johnson place, where my mind wandered a bit, and then downhill to Falls End. Mike had done some digging into some of the temporary residents of the camp, mainly the high school boys. There was nothing out of the way to re-port. Clean, upstanding young men one and all, guilty of nothing more than drinking beer under age and driving too fast on occasion. All-around all-American boys. With alibis for most of the other incidents. If you were inclined to believe parents, teachers, preachers, and the like. It was a policy of the Sher-iff's Department to do just that.

The car crunched over the gravel drive of Falls End and up to the general store. Haywood was inside, as usual. He'd graduated, though, to *Hustler* magazine.

"That won't make you go blind, Haywood, that'll give you a goddamn heart attack," I greeted him.

"What a way to go," he said, turning the magazine around in his hands, studying it from all angles. "Jesus, would you look at that!" he said, showing me the magazine. "Wouldn't hardly believe the human body could do that, now would you?"

I looked at the picture. I won't go into details. "Haywood, that's sick."

He grinned. "Yeah."

I took the offered beer as this was officially my day off, and drank long and hard. "You think this goddamn weather's ever gonna break?" I asked.

"Naw. Gonna stay this way till I'm dead, the way I figure," he answered.

"You think of anything you can tell me about that Monday? Mrs. Munsky?" I asked. It was a long shot.

"Naw. Nothin' more than I already told you, Milt, which was nothin'."

"Yeah. Sheriff's gonna make me let go of it pretty soon if I don't come up with something."

"Want me to make up something?" He grinned at me.

"Yeah. You wanna confess?" I thanked him for his hospitality and walked on out to my car.

This was my weekend on call and I wore my beeper on the hip opposite my holster and gun, making me look even wider than I was. Mountain Falls Road was outside of beeper range, so I figured I'd call the station as soon as I got close enough, but I didn't have to.

About three miles outside of Longbranch, the beeper went off. I pulled into a service station on Highway 5 and called in.

A.B. Tate was working that weekend and answered the phone.

"Hey, A.B. This is Milt. What's up?"

"Gotta call from Cleveland Davis out in Brancher! You know Cleveland?"

"Yeah, A.B., I know Cleveland. What'd he want?"

"Says a bunch of his cows is missing?"

"Yeah?"

"Thinks they been rustled?"

"Yeah." Since the price of beef went up, rustling has been on the upswing. Makes you feel like Matt Dillon going out to handle a call like that.

"Who's on this weekend 'sides you?"

"Dalton."

Wonderful. Between A.B. and Dalton, there might be enough brain power to figure out how to open a door.

"Okay, A.B. I'll go on up there, but when I do, I'll be outta beeper range again. Best call the sheriff and tell him."

"Okay, Milt. See ya."

I figured I'd call him from Cleveland's place just to make sure nothing untoward and puzzling had happened to the two deputies. Like somebody called or something.

I drove the twenty miles the other side of Longbranch to Cleveland Davis' place. Davis was my age and we'd gone to school together, playing on the same football team and basketball team. Cleveland had been the quarterback and the star forward. He'd let me hand him a towel every once in a while. Never did like Cleveland Davis.

His place in Brancher was big, a 1200-acre spread with some real good stock. It had been his wife's daddy's place which she inherited when the old man died. I'm not saying Cleveland married her for her daddy's land. The house was just an old farmhouse but it had been fixed up real nice. It was freshly painted white and I could see a new addition on the back. As I understood it, there was a Cleveland, Jr., doing great things on the Brancher High School football team and making some other kid feel inferior. What goes around comes around, as they say.

We shook hands cordially enough and then he started in on why there wasn't more coverage of the Brancher area by the Sheriff's Department. I tried to explain we only had so many people and a hell of a lot of territory to cover, and that if he and the other good people of the county would pass another bond election, maybe we might be able to hire enough deputies to go around.

"I'm tired of goddamn excuses, Milt, and I'm tired of having my cattle ripped off," Cleveland said. I hadn't seen him in a few years and was pleased to see he'd gained about twenty pounds. Looked downright pudgy. But prosperous. The cowboy hat on his head was suede and the band was of an expensive-looking hide, probably endangered. His boots looked endangered too. I was wondering if I could arrest him for that. His gut protruded over his belly, but not enough to hide the silver buckle.

We drove out to his pasture land in his Jeep, a brand-new custom job, and looked for clues. Just my luck, no matchbooks with a cryptic message inside.

"We'll do what we can, Cleveland," I said, after we'd gotten back to my car. Which we both knew would be next to nothing. You put out a flyer on the theft, you listened to see if any lowlifes in the county came into more money than they ought to have, and that was about it.

I drove on back to Longbranch and checked in at the station. Dalton and A.B. were playing Parcheesi. I was impressed.

"You boys doing okay?" I asked as I walked in.

They both looked up and grinned.

"Heya, Milt," Dalton said, and A.B. said, "How you?"

"You call the sheriff, A.B.?"

"Yeah. He said okay?"

"Okay what?"

"Okay that you go on up to Cleveland's and me and Dalton stay here and listen for the phone?"

"Oh."

"You find anything, Milt?" Dalton asked.

"Nary a thing. Same as usual."

We'd had three other rustlings in the county in the past year. I figured we'd find out who did it sooner or later. Maybe if they turned themselves in it might help.

"Well, boys, I'm gonna go on to the house. Just call me there and I'll turn off the beeper. Save the batteries."

Dalton grinned. "The county commissioners'll like that, Milt."

I grinned and waved and drove on home. Or to Mrs. Horne's house. Or whatever.

SIX

I GOT HOME and helped Mrs. Horne clean the screens. And I helped her weed-eat the backyard. And I helped her plow for her fall garden. And then I went in and thought about getting drunk. But as I'd done that the night before, I figured Aunt Merle might have a point and maybe I'd better not.

So I went to the store and bought cottage cheese, wheat bread, tuna fish, light beer, and Diet Coke. Time to get serious. Because serious was what I was getting about Laura Johnson. All the time I was helping Mrs. Horne and buying groceries I was thinking of ways to get back up to Mountain Falls Road. Because I knew that was what I was going to do. Even if she was married. Even if she had three little kids. And even if she thought I was just that nice, chubby, balding sheriff's deputy.

What I got back from the store, I checked in with Dalton and A.B. Nothing happening, so I sat down and opened a can of light beer. It tasted like piss and water. I got out my notebook and called the Tulsa Police Department and asked to talk to Detective Pruitt. He was off, wouldn't be on again until Monday at eight A.M. Nice job if you could get it. I left a message and drank some more of the piss and water. It grows on you.

And then I heard a scratching on my door. When I opened it, Evinrude was sitting there. Evinrude is a big, tiger-striped tomcat who'd adopted me the week I moved into my half of Mrs. Horne's house. I called him Evinrude because when he purred, which he did a lot, he sounded like an outboard motor. I hadn't seen him for four days.

"Well," I said, not moving to let him in. We have this relationship where I stay pissed at him and he forgives me for it. "I don't suppose there's a virgin left in Longbranch, now is there?"

He gave me one of those looks, stood up and walked around me into the apartment, where he jumped up onto my chair, curled into a ball, and fell asleep. After one of his rape-and-pillage excursions, he could sleep for four days straight. I picked him up and sat back down in my chair, putting him in my lap. I had work to do. I had to finish the piss and water.

Sunday I went to church with Mrs. Horne. Something I'd been meaning to do. The wife and I had gone to church Christmas, Easter, and Mother's Day, and it was a little strange hearing the preacher talk about something other than the special meaning of Christmas, Easter, or Mother's Day. Mrs. Horne had me over to Sunday dinner, which I thought was real nice, but I couldn't help thinking about that last Sunday dinner of Mrs. Munsky's. It had been almost a week now and no leads. A week-old murder is usually an unsolved murder as far as most police work goes. Least, so I've read in my journals.

I spent the rest of Sunday trying to get used to the light beer.

Monday morning, bright and early, I was in my office waiting for a phone call from Detective Pruitt. At eight-thirty, the call came.

"Kovak?"

"Yeah?"

"Pruitt. Tulsa."

"Yeah. How you doing? Thanks for returning my call so soon."

"Take it this is about the gallery people."

"Yeah. One of my informants I find may not be as reliable as I first thought. Hear she may be known to you people. Last name Murdock, first name Elsa. Lives next door to the Mayses."

"Just a minute."

He was gone for more like three, then came back on the line with a chuckle. "You got you a live wire there, Kovak. Looks like this lady has harassment complaints against her by at least three of her neighbors, and she's filed harassment complaints against everybody in Tulsa, including the mayor."

"Not what you'd call a reliable informant?"

"If the lady says the sun's shining, I'd be sure to carry an umbrella."

"Thanks, Pruitt. Talk to you later."

Talk about your bursting bubbles.

I spent the rest of the day with the sheriff going over the rustling incidents and trying to work out an investigative angle. I told him about my informant, Mrs. Murdock, and he just nodded his head. "What about the other neighbors?"

"Sir?"

"You interview the other neighbors?"

"Well . . . no, sir—I didn't."

"You think maybe that might be a good idea before you go saying Mrs. Murdock's full of shit? You think maybe confirmation is a two-way street? You think maybe the old lady lies maybe half the time but not all the time? You think maybe your old car can make another trip to Tulsa?''

I took the hint.

Tuesday, one week after the corpse of Mrs. Munsky was found, I was in Tulsa again. Diet or no diet, I went back to El Troja. In concession to the svelte figure I planned to become, I only had one basket of tostadas.

I drove to Dempler Drive and started with the neighbors on the other side of the Mayses'. They weren't home. The people directly across the street weren't home either. The house to the north of them was vacant and for sale, and at the house to the south, the people didn't know the Mayses from a hole in the wall. I asked if they'd noticed Blocker Mays's Mercedes there last week or David Perry's Volvo. They weren't looking, so who noticed? I kicked myself in the butt mentally for not asking around last week. With this much time passed, who'd remember?

That night, though, I found out who'd remember. I stayed in Tulsa late enough to wait for the neighbors to get home from work. When I went to the house across the street from the Mayses' I found a teenage boy, complete with bad complexion, bad haircut, and bad attitude.

"Excuse me, son," I said.

He looked up from the motorcycle he was working on. "Yeah?"

"You know the people across the street? Blocker and Kiersten Mays?"

"The short guy with the wife with the big tits?"

"Yeah."

"Yeah. I know 'em. Not to talk to, though. Why?"

I showed him my badge and ID. He wasn't impressed.

"You wouldn't happen to remember if they were home last weekend, would you? Not this past weekend, but the one before?"

"Yeah."

"Yeah, they were home?"

"Yeah, I happen to remember. She was, he wasn't."

"How come you can remember that so well?"

" 'Cause I like his car and I noticed I didn't see it from, jeez, Friday, I guess, till real late the next week. Tuesday, Wednesday, something like that. But I saw her." He grinned an evil grin. "Can't miss seeing that broad. You seen the tits on her?" I wondered what it was with this generation and big tits. But maybe that's just because I'm a leg man myself.

"Thanks for the information, son," I said. Confirmation number one.

I went to the house next door, on the other side from Mrs. Murdock's. I'd seen a car pull up to the garage while I was talking to the boy, a powder-blue Audi. The people in this neighborhood certainly were into foreign iron. Not a Ford or Chevy on the block that I could see. Downright un-American. The lady who answered the door was in her mid-to late twenties, pretty in a preppy sort of way, and well-dressed. I showed her my badge and ID and introduced myself.

She invited me in. It was a small house but furnished like a layout in a magazine. Or a model home. Not real cozy. I figured she spent money on her clothes, too. The skirt she was wearing was so long it had to be in fashion and her blouse looked like silk. But it's hard to tell these days, with all those synthetics around. But the belt around her waist was made of real silver and real turquoise, something I could recognize after my time in New Mexico.

I asked her the same question I'd asked the boy.

"Gosh, weekend before last? It's so hard to remember..." She paused and thought about it, then said, "Oh! That was the weekend my father was here visiting. Yes, I remember." She laughed. "I could hardly get him away from the fence all weekend! She was out there—Kiersten—in nothing, as usual, and Daddy—well—" She shrugged her shoulders and laughed with a kind of "boys will be boys" attitude.

"What about Mr. Mays? Did you see him at all?"

"Well, no, now that you mention it, I didn't. Maybe he wasn't home."

Yeah, maybe he wasn't. I thanked her and headed back to Prophesy County.

When I got back to the station, there was a message to call Laura Johnson whenever I got back. Time didn't matter. I called.

"Hi, Milt," she said when I'd identified myself. It was real cozy, the way she said "Hi, Milt." "I just wanted to say I was sorry I couldn't be more help to you the other day."

"Hey, I'm just sorry we didn't have the right guy for you to ID."

There was a small silence, then she said, "The kids really enjoyed the tour of the jail. And they liked you a lot, Milt."

"Well, they're real good kids, Laura." It felt great saying that, "Laura."

She laughed. "Yeah, they're something, aren't they?"

"Yeah," I agreed.

"They'd like to see you again. If you're ever up this way..."

"Well, as a matter of fact..."

"Yes?"

"I need to go see some people at Falls End tomorrow"—that was a bald-faced lie—"maybe I could come by?"

I could feel her smiling through the phone. "That would be great. How about lunch?"

"Oh, I don't want you to go to any trouble..."

"I have to fix lunch anyway, Milt. Fixing lunch for a man will be a nice break from peanut butter and jelly."

God, I liked the way she said that. I agreed to be at her house around noon the next day. Then I went home and wiled away my time in fantasyland.

I pulled into her driveway around eleven-thirty. I couldn't help myself. She was lucky I didn't show up at dawn. I remember after we hung up the phone that I really did need to get up to Mountain Falls Road, to see David Perry and confront him with the rest of the Mayses' neighborhood, so I felt a little better about the lie I'd told. Getting the message from her had temporarily caused amnesia about my second trip to Tulsa.

She was wearing a pair of baggy shorts that showed off beautiful freckled legs and a spaghetti-strapped top that showed off her great freckled shoulders. God, what legs. She was beautiful. No two ways about it. Her hair was pulled back from her face and up in the back with combs every which way. I started fantasizing about kissing the back of her neck. The back of her neck was beautiful.

The kids greeted me like their long-lost Uncle Milty, which I found I liked a lot. They were great kids. We ate at the picnic-type table in the kitchen and I was right—she did bake bread. At least it sure tasted like home-baked bread. Stuffed with chicken salad, with nuts in the salad. It was great. Not on my diet, I suppose, but great. And we all drank Kool-Aid and we all ended up with orange mustaches. It was the best lunch of my life.

Afterward, while Laura cleaned up the kitchen, the kids dragged me to the corral to admire their horses. There were three animals in the corral, two ponies and a horse. One pony was supposed to be Rebecca's.

"But I'm not gonna let her ride him anymore," Trent said seriously, "if she doesn't start grooming him better."

"You and what army's gonna stop me?" his little sister retorted. She reminded me a lot of my own little sister, who I hadn't seen in almost three years. I thought maybe I'd call her.

After a few minutes, I left the kids to their animals and went back into the house. Laura was finished with the kitchen and sitting in the living room with Adam. She smiled when I entered.

"Have a seat and I'll get you something a little stronger than Kool-Aid."

"Like a Coke?"

I followed her into the kitchen and helped get the drinks. I was more comfortable with this lady after one meal than I'd ever been with the wife after twenty-seven years.

"You're a nice man, Milton Kovak," she said, leaning against the kitchen counter and studying me with those turquoise eyes.

All that comfortableness went away and I felt like a teenager on his first date.

"Well, thank you kindly, ma'am," I said, trying to make a joke out of it.

"I mean it." She kept looking at me. I couldn't think of anything to say.

Finally, I said, "I almost bought this house once."

She smiled. "Really?"

I smiled back. "Yeah. But the wife didn't like it."

Her smile faded. I swear to God! "You're married?"

"Well, no. Not as of this past Monday. She divorced me. Divorce was final Monday."

She smiled again. "Now why would a woman divorce a man like you?"

I felt heat on my face and hoped I wasn't blushing. After all, I am a grown man, even if I did feel like a fourteen-year-old pimply-faced kid. "She had her reasons, I suppose," I answered, adding, "she didn't like this house, though. That's why we didn't buy it. I loved it."

She laughed. "Sounds like my husband and I may have had the same fight. I loved this house and he hated it. But I won. He still doesn't like it much."

God, the ties that bind!

"I guess my favorite room..." I started and she finished, "The room upstairs with all the windows?"

We both laughed. "Yeah," I said.

"Would you like to see it?"

"Yes, I would."

She walked out of the kitchen and into the living room, where the stairs led up to the second floor, picking up Adam off the living-room floor as she went.

"May I carry him?" I asked.

She smiled and handed me the baby. He looked at me and smiled and reached for my nose and said something that sounded like "dishwater," though I don't think that's what he meant. Wasn't appropriate somehow.

We went up the stairs, past the children's bedrooms to the door at the back, which entered the room with the windows. Laura had decorated it with woven wood blinds, now up all the way so you could see the view. There was an old couch even rattier than the one downstairs, with lots of giant throw pillows; a piece of old shag carpet covered the linoleum floor, and a TV stood in a place of honor in the room.

We sat down on the couch with Adam between us and looked out the windows to Tejas County between the twin peaks.

"God, this is great," I said. "Just like I remember it."

"We've been here three years and I haven't tired of the view yet. Guess I never will."

"When I first saw this room, I thought about how great it would be to sit here and watch a storm come up. You know?"

She smiled at me. "Yeah. I know. I've done it. It's—" She shrugged. "Well, the only word that pops to mind is erotic."

Erotic. Great word. I didn't say anything. Finally, she said, "Hey, Milt! Next time I see a storm brewing out there, how about I call you so you can come watch?"

Come and sit and watch an erotic storm with Laura Johnson? Not a bad idea, I thought. I smiled. "Yeah. That'd be great." I stood up. "Thanks again for lunch, Laura. It was great. But I'm a working man."

She picked up the baby and led me downstairs to the front door. "You're welcome here anytime, Milton Kovak. I hope you know that?" She was looking at me with that serious frown of hers, the turquoise eyes doing things to my soul.

"Well, that's very neighborly of you Laura," I said.

She took my hand in hers, in the one that wasn't holding on to the baby. "Nothing neighborly about it, Milt." I'm not going to say a word about the electric charge that went from her hand to mine that left my arm numb for a week. I won't even mention that. I smiled and walked through the screened-in front porch and waved good-bye to the kids out at the corral. They waved back and I left.

I know I needed just to turn to my left and head to David Perry's house. But in the state I was in, I wasn't sure how good an interrogation I could do. So I turned to the left all right, but ended up at Mrs. Munsky's house, where I just sat in the car in the heat of the August afternoon for about twenty minutes and thought about Laura Johnson.

Finally, I started the car, turned it around, and went to Perry's house. He was in and working and not too happy at the interruption.

"So, Milt, what is all this?" he said. "I thought we were finished?"

I walked past where he stood at the front door and went into the living room, taking a seat on the afghan-covered easy chair. He followed me in and sat on the sofa. I gave him my best hang-dog, sad-bassethound look and said, "David, I don't know why you did it. Don't know why Kiersten and Blocker did it either. But I'd surely like to know."

There was some sweat on his upper lip. He had the air-conditioning on so I figured it wasn't the August heat doing it. "What do you mean?"

I shook my head sadly. "You lied to me, David."

I think he was probably unaware that his tongue came out and licked at the sweat on his upper lip. Reminded me of an interview on TV once with a guy named Erlichman during the Watergate ballet. He laughed awkwardly. "I swear, Milt, I don't know what you're talking about."

"I'm talking, David, about the fact that Mrs. Murdock isn't the only neighbor that says you weren't at the Mayses' from Friday till Wednesday. I'm talking about the fact, David, that all the neighbors agree, David, that you weren't there, and neither was Blocker Mays. Now, David" —I went into my Baptist-preacher-consoling-an-errant-parishioner routine— "all I really want to know now is where you were and what you were doing? It's not nice to lie to the Sheriff's Department the way you been doing, David."

He stood up and he was shaking, either from anger or fear, and I was betting on fear. "Where I was is none of your fucking business, Kovak! Get out of my house." He pointed at the door. I felt like an unwed mother with babe in arms being thrown out in the snow. Sort of.

I walked to the door. "David," I said not unkindly, "I'm gonna find out where you were. And if you were here, and said you weren't, then I guess maybe you're gonna be a prime suspect in the murder of Mrs. Munsky."

He didn't say anything and neither did I. I just turned and walked to my squad car and got in and drove away. I'm a big believer in grand exits.

When I got back to the station, the sheriff was waiting for me at the door to his office. "There's been another one," he said by way of greeting.

"Rustling?"

He shook his head and ushered me into his office. "Last night. An old lady in Tejas County. Right on the boundary. Coulda been ours, but thank God she lived twenty feet over the line."

"Shit." I sank into one of his two visitor chairs and looked up at him as he crossed the room and sank into his chair.

He nodded his head. "She's right." He looked at me for a long moment, then sighed. "I don't like this, Milton. I don't like men coming into my county and hurting my people. I don't like murder and I don't like rape and I want it stopped. You hear me?"

"Yes, sir."

"What'ja got on that artist?"

So I told him.

"Haul him in."

"Sir?"

"Haul his ass in here."

"On what charge?"

He thought a minute, then smiled and said, "Withholding evidence in a capital crime. You like that?"

I smiled back. "I like that a lot."

So I went out to the deputy's bullpen and got Mike and took the squad car back up to Mountain Falls Road and read David Perry his rights and hauled his ass back down to Longbranch. It'd been a productive day.

SEVEN

"DAVID, I PERSONALLY don't think you did it," I said, shaking my head sadly. "I think you're covering for Blocker Mays, is what I think. I think he probably talked you into whatever little participation you had, David—"

"Fuck this," the sheriff said. "Let's just throw this asshole in jail and let the inmates talk to him." He grinned his evil grin. "You know they're gonna love buggering a guy that rapes and murders old ladies."

"Now, Sheriff," I said, sticking a small whine into my voice, "I really think David here is innocent. I think he just got pulled along—"

"I watch television," David Perry said, lighting a cigarette and throwing the match onto the Formica-topped table in front of them. "Good guy/bad guy, right? Personally, I think Cagney and Lacey do it better."

The sheriff leaned with his hands on the table, his face only inches away from Perry's. "Boy," he said, and the look in his eye was no act this time, "I don't like you. I don't like smart-mouthed Yankees moving into my county and doing bad. I don't like it at all. I don't like artsy-fartsy types who think the world owes 'em something because maybe they have a little God-given talent. I don't like bushy-haired, bearded boys who forget the sixties is long gone and the last hippie done died a natural death. In all, boy, I don't like you for anything but these murders. And I like you a lot for them. I think you done 'em, boy. And I got me a good cop here who's gonna prove it for me. You got that, boy?"

Perry flicked the ash from his cigarette in the general vicinity of the floor. Some of it, I noticed, landed on the sheriff's snake-skinned boot. I was getting a little worried for David Perry.

"Sheriff, how are you going to prove something that never happened? I wasn't here. I was in Tulsa. I don't care what those asshole neighbors of the Mayses say, I was there."

The sheriff grinned. "No, you wasn't, boy. 'Cause now it's three to three, and I gotta believe the three that ain't got no axes to grind or butts to save. I don't believe you. Or either of them Mayses. That clear, boy?"

Perry stood up abruptly, upsetting his chair. The sheriff caught it before it fell to the ground and grabbed Perry by the collar of his shirt. I stepped in. "Sheriff, how 'bout we put ole David here in one of the holding cells and see if we can't get Tulsa to pick up Blocker Mays? Sheriff?"

I didn't think he'd been listening. He was standing nose to chin with Perry, the crumpled-up shirt tight in his hand. Perry was looking hard at the sheriff and neither of them seemed to want to budge.

I stuck my elbow between them and gently pried them apart. "What'd ya say, Sheriff? And maybe Perry here needs to call a lawyer? What'd ya think?"

The sheriff let go abruptly and Perry almost lost his balance. I put a hand on his arm to steady him.

"Get this asshole out of my face, Milt."

"Sure thing, Sheriff."

I took the cigarette out of Perry's mouth and ground it on the floor under my foot, cuffed him, and led him out of the interrogation room and back to the holding cells.

"Milt, I didn't do this," Perry said as we walked down the short hall.

"Then maybe you'd better tell us where you were, David. Seems like the best thing to do."

He shut his mouth then and didn't say another word as I turned him over to the turnkey, instructing him to let Perry have his one phone call.

I walked back to my office, trying to ignore the rumbling in my stomach. It was after eight in the evening and I'd had nothing to eat since the chicken-salad sandwiches at Laura's. I walked into the sheriff's office.

"You okay, Elberry?" I hardly ever called him that, but the way he'd acted with Perry indicated a personal touch was needed.

"That's a slime bucket you got in there, Milton."

"Well, sir, maybe so, maybe not. But seems to me, Elberry, you got a little rough in there. Not like you at all."

He twirled around in his swivel chair to stare out the window. "I'm getting old, Milton. Too old for a job like this. I'm thinking maybe next election, I'm gonna just go fishing and forget the whole goddamn thing."

I wasn't too alarmed at this. The sheriff said that at least seven times a year. Just his way of letting off steam. So I said what I always said, "That'd leave the county in a pretty fix, now wouldn't it?"

He swiveled the chair back to face me. "I think I'm serious this time. I'm fifty-seven years old, Milton. I been screwing around with assholes like that slime you got in there for almost thirty years. I'm getting tired of always wanting to take a bath."

I leaned forward and looked earnest. "Sheriff, we're gonna find out what's going on here. Whoever it is doing this, whether it's Perry or not, we're gonna find 'em. And we're gonna put 'em away and then you'll feel a whole lot better."

He smiled a sad smile. "I hear your stomach rumbling, Milton. You go on home to supper now, okay?"

"Yes, sir. Good advice for you too."

"Yeah."

But he just sat there, twirling around and around in his swivel chair and I thought for the first time in my nearly twenty years as sheriff's deputy that maybe this next election, Elberry Blankenship's name would not be on the ballot. Which is sorta akin to waking up in the morning and finding out the sun burned up while you were asleep. Not a real good feeling.

It was as close to dark as you could get and still see when I pulled up to Mrs. Horne's house. As I got out of the car and walked up to the porch of my half of the house, she came walking around the side.

"Mr. Kovak?"

I smiled. "Hey, Miz Horne. How you doing?"

She smiled in return. "Kinda late getting home, aren't you? Any new developments on Mrs. Munsky?"

"None I can talk about, ma'am. Sorry."

She shook her head. "Don't be. I'm not meaning to butt into your business, Mr. Kovak. Actually, reason

I came around, your wife called a while ago. Needs to talk to you right away."

I groaned inwardly. "Thanks, Miz Horne. I'll call her right back." Which, of course, I didn't. I let myself in and took off my shoes and popped the top on a light beer and sat down in my chair with the lights still off in the apartment. I didn't want to think about the wife, or David Perry, or the sheriff maybe not being the sheriff any longer. All I wanted to think about was Laura Johnson. But the gods wouldn't let me do that, because no sooner had I sat down and thought her name to myself than the phone rang. It was the wife.

"Milton?"

"Hey."

"Milton . . ." I could tell something was wrong.

"Honey? What is it?"

Then she began to cry for real. In between the sobs, I heard, "It's Uncle Fred. He'd dead."

A wave of tenderness I hadn't felt in a long time washed over me. I wished for just a moment that she wasn't on the phone, but here, where I could put my arms around her and hold her. "Ah, baby," I said. "I'm so sorry. What happened? I thought it was just sunstroke?"

"He had a heart attack in the hospital. They couldn't save him."

"Honey, you want me to come over there? You at your mama's?"

"No, Milt. Don't come over. There's no need. I just wanted you to know. They're laying him out at Floyd's tonight. Viewing tomorrow. Funeral's gonna be on Friday. Can you come to that?"

"Sure, honey. I'll be there. And I'll go by Floyd's tomorrow. Your mama okay?"

"No, not really. Her only brother, ya know?"

"Yeah, I know. How's Aunt Merle?"

"Under sedation. She took it real hard."

Yeah, I thought. Who's she gonna boss around now? I had a feeling I knew why Uncle Fred had been up on that roof in the noonday August sun anyway. Farthest place away from Aunt Merle he could get. But, of course, I didn't say that.

"If you need anything..."

"No. We're okay. Some people from Mama's church have been around with some food. We're doing okay. I just... well..."

"Yeah, baby, I know."

"We're divorced now, Milton."

"Yeah, I know."

"Doesn't feel much different, does it?"

"Naw. The sun still came up and everything."

"Maybe we shouldn't've done it."

"Honey—"

There was a long silence. Then a sniff. "I'm sorry. That was stupid. Good-bye, Milton."

She hung up before I had a chance to say good-bye. I sat there on the couch for a long time, long after the first light beer was nothing but a piss-flavored memory, and thought about my wife, my marriage, and my divorce.

God, she'd been a pretty little thing. A sophomore when I was a senior. Quiet, soft-spoken. The type nobody much paid any mind to. Except me. And maybe I wouldn't have either except that she broke the strap on one of her shoes while she was walking in front of me up the stairs of the school.

That was in October of my senior year. I was a semipopular football player, making a few points for the team every year, but not exactly star quality, you know what I mean? Not big enough to have any girl I chose. Not even big enough to get a date very often. And then she broke the strap on her shoe and lost her balance and fell and I caught her. She'd been a tiny little thing. She'd felt like a kitten in my arms. And she blushed. When she was walking home from school that afternoon, I skipped football practice to follow her and offer her a ride in my '55. She accepted.

Maybe if we'd had kids, things would have worked out. Maybe if we'd had kids she wouldn't have turned so bitter somewhere along the way. Or maybe I was the one who was bitter. I don't know. But it was over. She knew it and I knew it and everybody in Longbranch knew it. I wondered if she'd start dating, and the thought of that made my stomach turn over. I couldn't see her with another man. I doubt if she could either. She'd never even dated before the day that she broke the strap of her shoe. And she'd been a virgin when we lay together that first night of our marriage in the old bed my mama and daddy had given us, in that room over the garage of my parents' house. Just two weeks out of the Air Force. And we'd both cried. I can admit that now. It's okay now for a man to say he cried. Hell, it's downright masculine to say that now. But then, it had been our secret.

I sat there in the dark living room and let the tears run down my cheeks and I wondered if I still loved her. And if I didn't, when had I stopped? And why? And when had she stopped loving me? I fell asleep in the old easy chair with Evinrude in my lap and the doors and windows still unlocked.

And woke up in the morning with a crick in my neck and my mouth tasting like used kitty litter. I called the Sheriff's Department and told Gladys about Uncle Fred and that I'd be in late that morning, then took a shower, shaved, brushed my teeth till the gums bled, and dressed up in my only dark suit. It was wool and scratchy and I knew by late afternoon, if I didn't change into something lighter, I'd be sweating like David Perry's upper lip. But there are traditions, and a new ex-husband had to be careful about appearances.

Floyd Ackerman owned the funeral parlor in town. Oh, there were other funeral parlors, owned by upstarts or conglomerates, but if you wanted to be buried with style and tradition, you went with Floyd or a Hefty Lawn and Leaf bag. The funeral home was in what used to be, back before the turn of the century, a private residence. It was three stories high and about a block long and was built in the best tradition of Western Gothic. The public viewing areas and chapel were on the first floor, the messy stuff in the basement, the offices on the second floor, and Floyd's residence on the third. He and Lois had raised three kids on the third floor of the funeral home, and as far as I knew, none of them had grown up to be a necrophiliac.

I walked into the foyer in my scratchy dark suit and was greeted by Floyd's oldest son, Marvis, who, like his daddy, was razor-thin, with no chin to speak of, and big, sad brown eyes. He took my offered hand and shook it warmly, a sad smile playing across his hollow-cheeked face.

"Milton, my condolences."

"Thank you, Marvis. How's your daddy?"

"Just fine. He's with the widow now." He pointed toward a door on the left. "You want to view the deceased?"

"Thank you."

I walked to the door and opened it, steadying myself for Aunt Merle and the boys. The room was empty of everyone but the deceased and Aunt Merle. She was sitting in a folding chair by the coffin, her ample buttocks sagging over both sides, knitting in hand. The look on her face when she saw me was stern. Of course, I don't remember ever seeing any other look on Aunt Merle's face.

"Milton."

"Aunt Merle." I nodded at her and walked up to the deceased, namely Uncle Fred.

"Don't he look natural?" Aunt Merle said.

"Um-hum," I said. Actually, he didn't. I've never seen a dead body that did. He looked like a wax dummy. Actually, once, in the Air Force, I got out to Los Angeles and went to the wax museum there. They had a dummy there made to look like John Wayne. That dummy looked a lot more lifelike than Uncle Fred did at that moment. But I didn't say so.

A side door opened and Floyd Ackerman walked in with Aunt Merle's boys, Jesse, the used-car salesman, and Teddy Joe, the Bishop Junior High basketball coach. They both took after their mama in looks, manner, and disposition. I'd always considered the boys to be total assholes. I supposed they'd been in the back room with Floyd paying up for their daddy's funeral. With Floyd, dying nice came with a mighty choice price tag.

"Milton," Teddy Joe said, nodding toward me.

"Teddy Joe."

Jesse held out his hand. "Milton."

"Jesse." We shook. "Sorry about your daddy."

"Thank you."

We all just stood there looking at what was left of Uncle Fred. There didn't seem to be a whole lot to say. Finally, the little song and dance ended when the front door opened and the wife and her mother came in.

The lady I'd lived with for twenty-seven years came up and shook my hand. I swear to God. Her mother didn't even look my way.

"Thanks for coming by, Milton," she said.

"Least I could do."

"Don't he look natural?" her mother said to the room in general. She was standing by the coffin that held her big brother, looking down at him with sad eyes. For some reason, I again thought of my own baby sister. Thinking twice about her in the same week made me know for certain I'd better call.

"Well, I'd best be getting on to the station," I said to anybody who might be listening.

The wife turned and looked at me. I saw her for a moment as she used to be, that tiny little girl with the broken shoe strap. Then the image faded and she was just a middle-aged lady with sagging breasts and thin hips. Somebody I used to know.

"Bye, Milt."

"Bye." And I knew that this was the real one. That the marriage was over. More final now than any divorce could make it. I was no longer part of this family, and showing up here, or at the funeral, would not make me part. I knew I'd go to the funeral just the same, for appearances and because I'd always liked Uncle Fred, but just as one of the mourners, standing in the back, not part any longer. It made me sadder than anything I could think of. I left.

It was only a little after nine in the morning when I walked outside but it was hotter than blazes and the sky was that sort of whitish blue it gets when you know the world's going to stay hot for the rest of your life. I decided to stop by Mrs. Horne's house to change out of the wool suit before heading back to the station.

I was stripped down to shirt and shorts and standing in front of the window air conditioner when I decided to call Jewel. Jewel's my little sister. She lives with her husband Henry and their three children in Houston and the last time I'd seen her was at our mama's funeral three years before. We'd argued about what to do with Mama's house and the visit hadn't been a pleasant one.

We'd never been particularly close. I had been thirteen when Jewel was born and I hadn't liked it a bit. For one thing, it was embarrassing to have a pregnant mother when you're that age. For another, I'd had my parents all to myself for thirteen years. And then she came along. Pretty and tiny and sweet and she just made me look all the more awkward. I hadn't really paid much attention to her, and when I left home she was barely five years old. I hadn't had much to do with her until Daddy died. I'd already been with the Sheriff's Department for a few years and Jewel was in her third year of college at Norman when Daddy died and she had rebelled from it in the only way girls had in those days. She got pregnant. And I did something I wished I'd never done. She called me and told me because she was afraid and didn't know what to do. And I was her big brother. So, for the first time in our relationship, I did something.

I went to Norman and told her she had to marry the boy for Mama's sake. Mama couldn't take it, I'd told her. Not this on top of Daddy dying. The only decent thing for Jewel to do, I told her, was marry the boy. I was a real pompous ass about it too. It's one of those memories you have that you don't feel right proud of.

The boy had been Henry, I guess the easiest guy to seduce. Because he wasn't much else. Myopic, small, with a tremor in his hand when he shook mine. And she didn't love him and she didn't want to marry him. She just wanted it all to go away. But I'd said no. She had to marry him. And I guess because Daddy was dead and I was the only authority figure she had, she did it. But I guess it hadn't been all that bad. They'd been married now for sixteen years and had three kids and Henry was an accountant for an oil company in Houston.

I had to look up her number in my little personal phone directory. I didn't call her often enough to have it memorized. Actually, I don't think I've called her more than three times in the ten years she's lived there, and all three times had to do with Mama. Mama's in the hospital, Mama's dying, Mama's dead.

She picked up the phone on the third ring.

"Jewel? It's Milt."

"Milt? Oh. Hi."

"How you doing?"

"Fine. How're you?"

"Fine."

"Anything wrong?"

"No. No. Everything's just fine. I just . . . well, I've been thinking about you a lot lately."

"Oh? Why?"

I don't know what I expected. Maybe that she'd be happy to hear from me. I don't know.

"I got a divorce. Well, rather, she did."

"I know. She called me."

"Oh?"

"Yeah. Couple of months ago. Said she'd left you."

"Oh."

"You okay?"

"Yeah. I guess."

"I'm just glad Mama's not alive to see this. You know how she felt about divorce."

What goes around comes around.

"Well, Jewel, how's Henry?"

"He's fine."

"And the kids?"

"They're just fine. Leonard's gonna be in band this year, playing the tuba, can you believe it? And Marlene's going out for the drill team. But the girl's got two left feet, so I doubt she's gonna make it. And, Milton, you're not going to believe this, but Carl's going into junior high!"

"No kidding?"

I'd forgotten the name of her youngest child. I felt bad about that. I felt bad about a lot of things.

"Jewel?"

"Yes?"

"We're family, right?"

She laughed. "Well, Mama always denied you were adopted, even though I kept saying you had to be!"

"Family needs to keep in touch."

There was a silence. Finally she said, "You're right, Milton. You and I, we're all we have left, I guess."

"Maybe I can—I don't know, come see you sometime, or something?"

"Here? Come to Houston?"

"Maybe."

"Well, Milt, we'd love to have you, but the kids are getting so big now and they're so busy—and the house just keeps getting smaller and smaller..."

"Well, maybe you and Henry will come back to Longbranch for a visit."

"Of course! That would be great! But school's starting and it's so hard to get away..."

"Christmas?" Why did I keep trying? What did I think I was doing?

"Oh, I wish we could! I really do. But Henry's mama's coming Christmas to stay with us."

"Well, maybe some other time."

"Sure, Milt. That'd be great."

"Right. Great." Another of those big silences filled the long-distance air.

"Jewel, it was real good talking to you, but I gotta get to work."

"Well, you keep in touch now, Milt, you hear?"

"Right. Bye."

There are times in a man's life when he's damned lucky he uses an electric razor, you know what I mean? This was one of those times. I put on my rumpled seersucker suit and left for the station.

EIGHT

WHEN I GOT TO the station, David Perry was gone. Blocker Mays and a Tulsa lawyer had got him out that morning. I went in to see the sheriff.

"Morning, Sheriff," I said as I knocked and entered his office.

"Milt." He looked up from some papers on his desk. "Goddamn JP wouldn't give us a writ on Perry. Not enough evidence. Asshole's walked and there ain't a goddamn thing we can do about it."

"Yes, sir, that's what I hear."

"You don't like Perry for it, do you?" The look on his face was plain accusatory.

"Well, sir, no, not exactly."

"Why?"

"I'm not saying the guy's clean, 'cause he's not. He's lying about something. But I just don't think he did it."

"Who you know you think could rape and strangle an old lady?"

"Sir?"

"Who you know would wave their dick at some little kid walking home from school?"

"Sheriff, I think I see the point you're trying to make—"

"The point I'm trying to make, Milton"—and here his voice started getting loud—"is that there ain't no way you can know by looking at someone, by talking with someone, by going to *church* with someone, what they're capable of doing. One thing I've learned in thirty years doing this goddamn work, Milton, is that people're all basically assholes. Every goddamn one of 'em.''

''Yes, sir.''

''Now go find me a rapist. And if you can't do that, find me a goddamn rustler. Okay?''

I left his office. The sheriff was pissed, there was no doubt about that, and I didn't figure on sticking around to get any more of the brunt of it. But I still didn't like Perry for it.

I spent the rest of that Thursday making phone calls, checking flyers, and doing all those boring things a deputy does when there are no leads in a case. And I not only had no leads in one case, I had no leads in two cases.

Friday was Uncle Fred's funeral. Luckily, it was being held in the morning, so I put on my scratchy wool suit and went to the Lutheran church where the services were being held, and then drove my '55 to the cemetery where I stood outside of the awning, away from the family, and said my own kind of good-byes to Uncle Fred. I nodded to a few people and shook hands with Aunt Merle's boys. There was a goodly sized crowd, as Uncle Fred had been a popular man. And the people at Aunt Merle's church would've no more not shown up than they would have stripped naked and gone to the K Mart. I saw Aunt Merle looking around and imagined her mentally writing down the names of those not in attendance. I prayed to God that they be spared.

After the services, I went back to Mrs. Horne's house, changed back into the seersucker that I knew would have to go to the cleaner's pretty soon, fed Evinrude, since I'd forgotten to do it before I left, then headed back to the station.

I had a bee in my bonnet. I wanted to know where David Perry had been that Monday. Actually, I wanted to know where he'd been from Friday until the next Wednesday. I didn't think he'd been hiding out somewhere waiting for the right moment to jump poor Mrs. Munsky. I just couldn't see it, no matter what the sheriff said. But he had to be somewhere. And so did Blocker Mays. And wherever they had been, they had been together, that was obvious. So what could two men do together? Go fishing? Hunting? But why be so secretive? Catting around? Then why had Kiersten Mays lied for them? Most wives get mighty pissed off when their husbands and their buddies go catting around. I figured it was something illegal. Dope. Stolen art. I don't know. What could an artist and a gallery owner be into? I figured the best way to start was to call New York, where I knew Perry was from, and see if they had anything on him.

Now, normally, calling the NYPD out of the blue would get you exactly nowhere. Their caseload being what it is, they don't have a lot of time for hick deputies calling up and bending their ears. But I happened to have an in on the NYPD and her name was Reba Logan. We had dated a few times while we were both stationed at White Sands in New Mexico. And when I confessed that I was engaged to a girl back home and felt guilty as homemade shit for going out with her, she confessed that she was gay, and it was the start of one of the best friendships I had in the Air Force.

Reba wasn't my idea of a lesbian. I guess when I was growing up, after I figured out what one was, I had the impression they were all these huge, hairy women with too many male hormones who wore T-shirts with cigarette packs rolled up in the sleeves and said "fuck" a lot. Well, Reba did say "fuck" a lot, but since then I've met a lot of women, feminine types, who say "fuck" a lot, so I guess that saying it doesn't have anything to do with who you do it with, if you know what I mean. But Reba wasn't the stereotypical, so to speak, lesbian. She was small and dark and downright pretty. And the only thing masculine about her was the way she could roll a cigarette with one hand. I never could do that.

So I called Reba Logan in New York.

"Milton Kovak! I'll be goddamned! What're you up to?" She sounded just like she used to. Full of life and ready to fight. God, what a woman. She'd escaped her hometown in Mississippi at the ripe age of seventeen, two months after discovering that she didn't like boys, and run off to join the Air Force. We'd both been discharged at the same time. She came back to Longbranch with me to attend the wedding. The wife hated her on sight, even after I told her Reba's sexual leanings. She just changed her mind about Reba being after my firm young flesh and decided she was after her own sweetness.

"My asshole in alligators, if you wanna know the truth," I answered.

"I thought you lived in Oklahoma, not Florida."

"Is that some kind of New York humor?"

"Not much of it. I don't want to tire your poor hick brain."

"Got a problem here, Reba, maybe you can help out."

"Let Reba's flying fingers case your aching whatever."

"You still working computers?"

"I'm as user-friendly as you can get."

"You talking computerese to this country boy?"

"I'll go get a translator if you need."

"Can you pull up a sheet on somebody for me? Not even sure if he has one."

"Shoot."

"Name's David Perry. An artist. Used to live up your way...oh, about three, four years ago."

"Hold it."

I heard her mumbling to herself and heard the click of her fingers on the keyboard.

"Seventeen outstanding parking tickets issued to a David Perry at an address in the village. Your boy?"

"Yeah, but we ain't worried about where he parks. Unless it's in old ladies' driveways."

"Huh?"

So I explained.

"Goddamn fucking assholes. As far as I'm concerned, Milt, with the exception of you and one other man I met once, the whole lot of your sex could be strung up by the balls and the world would be a better place."

"Well, I ain't gonna argue the point, Reba, 'cause you may be right."

"So, anything else on the case before we start telling each other lies about how great we are?"

"Yeah. It's a long shot, but what the hey…Blocker Mays…M-A-Y-S…and while you're at it, Kiersten Mays…K-I-E-R-S-T-E-N."

"Hold on."

I heard the click of the keys, then a muttered "Well, goddamn!" then more keys clicking. She kept me there at least five minutes before she came back on the line.

"Hold on to your dick, Milton. As you used to say too damn often, we got us a sick puppy here."

"Who?"

"Blocker. Got a sheet longer than you—well, a lot longer than your…" She giggled.

"Well, just keep my…out of it, okay?"

"Two pops for aiding to the delinquency of minors, one for child molestation, three soliciting (he's buying, not selling). All little boys. Also got pulled in at a raid way back when—back when gays couldn't meet at a bar without getting hassled, but that's another story."

"Well, interesting, but little boys and old ladies seem mighty diversified."

"Now wait. We haven't got to sweet Kiersten yet."

"She's got a sheet too?"

"Soliciting—selling, not buying—four pops for that, one conviction. Two petty thefts, looks like johns that complained but wouldn't press charges. And a deportation proceeding that took place in 1983. All under the name of Kiersten Banaczek, which cross-references to Kiersten Mays. They dropped the deportation because she married an American citizen."

"Namely Blocker Mays."

"You got it."

"Okay." I wrote as fast as I could in my book, using what I call shorthand but what is more like illegible abbreviations. "So, what we got here is an artist who can't park properly, a pederast, and a hooker. That the way you see it?"

"What's a pederast?"

"That's the name for a man that messes with little boys."

"Jesus H. Christ! They got a name for it? That's sick!"

"Yeah, but—"

"You know what's the sickest part, Milton?"

"What's that, Reba?" I sighed. Reba could go on a bit when she wanted.

"The sickest goddamn part, Milton, is that there's a name for it. And you know why there's a name for it, Milton?"

"Why's that, Reba?"

"Because men write the fucking dictionaries, that's why! Not only do they do it, they gotta make up a name for it! That's fucking sick, Milton!"

I agreed and we went on a bit about the rottenness of men in general and Noah Webster in particular before I could get her back to the case at hand.

"So," I finally said, "what we got is three people, two of whom aren't what you'd call your model citizens. Right?"

"Yeah. So what's the connection to your case?"

"Goddamned if I know." I thought for a moment, then said, "Hey, Reb, you know I'm divorced now?"

"No shit? When'd this happen?"

"Officially this past Monday."

"So, you running all the ladies of Longbranch wild?"

"If I am, they haven't noticed yet."

"You handling it?"

"If I am, I haven't noticed yet."

She laughed. Reba always had this great laugh. "Milty, if I didn't have a special friend right now who's the jealous type, I'd fly right down there and see what I've been missing all these years."

"Yeah, well, save the plane fare, Reba. I'm afraid you haven't been missing much."

"You gonna be one of these poor-mouth types? 'If she divorced me it proves I'm no good?' Can't stand that type, Milt. Makes me want to puke, you know?"

I laughed. "You're right. I think I got me a case of feeling sorry for myself. But it'll pass."

"It better. 'Cause the one thing I always liked most about Milton Kovak, he was one of the few people I ever knew who liked being with himself. You know?"

"Yeah. Reba..."

"Yeah?"

"Good talking to you."

"You too, Milt."

I hung up the phone and stared at it for a full five minutes. Yeah, I had a case all right. Poor Milton. No wife. Few friends. No one to carry on the great Kovak name. Almost forty-eight years old, and living like a goddamn monk. So I sat there and thought about Laura Johnson. Somehow, it helped.

And, of course, the phone rang. It was Bill Williams from Tejas County.

"Milt, think we found your green Chevy."

"No shit? Where?"

"Abandoned about two miles from the house of the last old lady. You wanna bring your witness to ID it?"

"You find the guy?"

"No such luck. Just a dead car."

"Yeah, okay, Bill. Where you want me to meet you?"

He gave me directions to the location of the car, and I hung up and dialed Laura Johnson's number. She answered on the third ring.

"Laura? It's Milton Kovak."

"Hi, Milt, how are you?" I could see her smiling at the mention of my name. It was doing things to me that could be embarrassing in the station house.

"I've got another ID for you, Laura. This time just the car, though."

"Oh. Sure. When?"

"As soon as possible. I'll come pick you up."

"The kids and I will be ready by the time you get here. Where are we going?"

"Tejas County. Just over the line."

"Okay. I'm looking forward to seeing you, Milt."

And what do you say to a line like that?

Mountain Falls Road was on the way from Long-branch to Tejas County, so it worked out just fine. If it had been twenty miles out of my way, it still would have worked out just fine.

Little Rebecca came running out of the house as I pulled up and jumped into my arms as I got out of the car. I hugged her and ruffled her big brother's hair and felt wonderful. Laura came out with her purse, diaper bag, and baby in her arms. When Adam saw me, he reached out for me, I swear to God. I set Rebecca down and took the baby to relieve Laura of some of the burden. We all piled into the squad car and headed for Tejas County.

It was only a ten-mile drive, a hell of a lot closer than Longbranch, and we only had time enough to catch up on everybody's week and what new school clothes they had gotten, and how wonderful kindergarten was going to be. Trent, as an aging second grader, sat back in his seat, smug in his knowledge, and let his little sister babble on and on about the joys and fears of going to school for the first time. Would her teacher be pretty? Would the other kids laugh at her because she still couldn't say her *r*'s properly? Would there be enough food to go around at lunchtime? Would the teacher throw her out because sometimes she forgot and said "elemenopee" like it was one word?

Laura and I reassured her like an old married couple, and I felt peaceful and happy for the first time since my lunch with this bunch. I knew I was heading for serious trouble, but it was full steam ahead.

I pulled off Highway 5 at FM 217, went 2.7 miles by the odometer, took a left onto an oiled-clay side road, drove .35 miles and turned left again onto a rutted dirt road. The grass growing up in the middle of the two tire tracks was so high it was obvious the road wasn't used often, if at all. A few yards down the dirt road, I spotted the Tejas County sheriff's car and the green Chevy pulled over on the verge, half hidden under the spread of a weeping-willow tree. Bill Williams walked out from under the shade of the tree as we pulled up.

The opposite side of the road from where the car was parked was fenced with barbed wire, behind which grazed some very sedate bovine types. Trent and

Rebecca jumped out of the car as soon as it was stopped and headed for the fence to talk to the animals. Laura, with Adam in her arms, and I got out to greet Bill.

Bill Williams was a big old boy. He'd played ball for OU for a couple of years back in the fifties before his grades and the draft got to him. I'd known Bill professionally for about ten years and he wasn't a bad cop. He had a tendency, though, to take things at face value. Something I never could do. I've got to look under the rock and see what's squirming.

Bill and I shook hands and I introduced him to Laura.

"Sorry to call you out like this, Miz Johnson," he said, "but I thought maybe we might have something here."

He pointed to the car and Laura walked over to it, looked at it, walked around it. It was a green Chevy, all right. A '73. With a ripped and faded black vinyl top.

Laura shook her head as she came back to join Bill and me.

"I don't know," she said. "It could be. But maybe not." She shook her head again and looked sad. "I'm sorry. I guess I'm not all that great with cars."

"It fits the description Milt here gave me," Bill insisted.

Laura nodded. "Yes, I know, but—" She turned and looked at it again. "There was something hanging—" She turned and looked at me. "You know, like those oversized fuzzy dice people have in their cars? Something like that. Something hanging off the rearview mirror."

Bill looked at me. "You never mentioned that."

Laura smiled apologetically. "Because I didn't mention it to him. I just remembered it."

"Well, those things come off. That doesn't mean this ain't the same car."

Laura moved Adam from one hip to the other. "I know." She looked at Bill and shook her head again. "I am sorry, really. But I just can't say positively that this is the car I saw."

"But you can't say positively it isn't, either, right?" he asked.

She shrugged. "That's true, I guess."

He thanked us in an offhand kind of way and we bundled the kids back in the car and headed back to Mountain Falls Road.

Once there, she invited me inside for a glass of iced tea. The thought of not going in never crossed my mind. It was already late afternoon and nothing much was happening at the station. I saw no reason to drive the eighteen miles back in some sort of hurry to sit around and stare at my empty desk, when I could sit around and stare at Laura.

"Okay if I use the phone?" I asked her. "I need to call the station. Tell 'em I won't be coming back in."

"Sure." She smiled and pointed at the phone on the round, three-tiered table by the front window of the living room. "I'll get the tea."

As I started toward the phone, it rang. Laura walked around me to get to it, brushing against me as she did so. I could smell her, she was so close. Not a perfumey smell, but a natural smell of soap, shampoo, and clean. It took some effort not to reach out to her as she passed.

"Hello? Oh, hi. But I've got dinner all planned. Whatever. What time? Okay. I guess I'll see you when I see you. Bye."

She put the phone down and stared out the front window toward the corral for a moment, then turned abruptly to me, a smile on her face.

"Will you stay for dinner?" she asked.

"Ah."

"That was my husband. He won't be home until late and he's going to eat on the road. So, will you stay for dinner?"

She had crossed her arms and was leaning against the window, looking at me with that frank expression of hers.

"Sure, I'd love to." I smiled. She smiled. We just stood there smiling at each other and I, for one, felt like a fool. A very happy fool.

She pushed herself away from the wall and headed for the kitchen. "Okay. That's settled. Hope you like chicken?"

"I love chicken," I said to her retreating back. I called the station.

While Laura cooked I played a rousing game of Candy Land with Trent and Rebecca, spending most of my time trying to keep Adam from eating the small pieces of the game. I lost. Dinner was broiled chicken and new potatoes and a salad. It was the best dinner I'd ever eaten. With homemade bread to go with it. Afterward, Laura and I cleaned the kitchen together while the big kids watched TV and Adam sat on the floor of the kitchen playing with a pot and spoon. She gave him a wooden spoon to keep the noise level down.

Then Laura took Adam upstairs to get him ready for bed and I read a story to the two older kids. I felt I belonged as I'd never felt before. I tried not to remember that this was another man's family.

"Okay, buckaroos, time to hit the bunkhouse," Laura said as she came down the stairs.

"God, I hate it when she talks cowboy," Trent said with a laugh.

Laura grabbed him around the waist and lifted his legs up into the air. "This town's not big enough for the two of us, pardner. I'll meet you outside in the street. Six-guns at twenty paces," she said.

Rebecca sat in my lap, laughing at her mother and big brother. I laughed too.

"Piggyback me to bed?" Rebecca asked me, turning those bright eyes so like her mother's on me.

"You bet," I said, swinging her off my lap, standing, and swinging her onto my back.

In fifteen minutes, they were snug in their rooms while their mother and I sat in the many-windowed room of the second floor, the door closed so our conversation wouldn't disturb the children.

"Do you have children, Milt?" Laura asked.

"No. The wife and I were never blessed with any, I'm sorry to say."

"That's a shame. You'd have made a great father."

I smiled. "Thank you."

She looked out a window into the darkness beyond. She laughed ruefully. "Sometimes I wish my kids had a father. What they have is a big brother. And what I've got is four kids instead of just three."

I didn't say anything. I didn't know what to say.

"Milt, would you think it awful of me if I asked you something?"

"I would never think anything you did was awful, Laura. Ask away."

She looked at her feet and said quietly, "Would you be my friend? Would you come by here sometimes just to say hi? Just have lunch? Could I call you just to talk?"

She turned and looked out the window again. As if she were trying to look anywhere but at me. "I am your friend, Laura," I said. I could feel the flush creep up my face. "And I'd like to do that."

She turned to face me, and with that serious beautiful frown of hers, she said, "I like you, Milton Kovak. I like you a hell of a lot."

I stood up. "Well, thank you, Laura. I like you a hell of a lot, too. But I've got to go."

And I did.

NINE

MAYBE IT WAS REBA, or maybe it was Laura, or maybe it was just me, but that weekend I got my act together. I went out and bought a secondhand sofa. And a coffee table, end table, two lamps, and an electric frying pan. And on Saturday, I took the seersucker suit to the cleaner's, bought a new shirt and sports jacket and two pairs of slacks. I got my hair cut and had the first manicure of my life. I called up an old friend and met him for drinks at the Longbranch Inn, and smiled and greeted Glenda Sue like the old friend she was instead of like the guilt I was carrying around in my back pocket.

On Sunday, I went to church with Mrs. Horne for the second time in a row, had Sunday dinner with her, fixing the salad myself, and spent all Sunday afternoon working with her in her fall garden.

By Monday morning, I had a sore back, new clothes, and a cleansed soul. Milton Kovak was back with a vengeance.

Sitting at my desk in my office, I went over my notes on Mrs. Munsky's murder. A lot of notes. Not one of them meaning a goddamn thing. The one thread I hadn't pulled all the way out yet was still good old David Perry. I had an idea now, after my talk with Reba, about what David and Blocker had been doing over that weekend, if not where. I drove up to Mountain Falls Road and pulled into David Perry's drive.

"My lawyer's going to sue you people for harassment, Kovak," he said by way of greeting.

"I'm just fine, David," I said, letting myself in, "how about you?"

"You can take your so-called redneck humor and shove it up your ass," he said, following me into his living room.

I sat down in the easy chair and looked up at him. Some people think looking up at somebody puts them at a disadvantage. It doesn't bother me at all. Makes me feel all "ah shucks" and Colomboish, if you know what I mean.

"How long you and Blocker Mays been lovers, David?"

Now that did take him by surprise. He sat down. "What in the fuck are you talking about?"

"You wanna tell me where you two lovebirds were hiding out that weekend?"

"I want you to get the fuck out of my house," he said, but he didn't move.

"Now there's no law in Oklahoma against that, not right now anyway. Used to be, not anymore. Unless, of course, you two were playing around with little boys. I know how Blocker likes that."

He stood up. "Get out."

I stood up and pushed him back down. I was getting fed up. "Jesus, David. The sheriff wants to lock your ass up for raping and strangling old ladies. And you were out humping Blocker Mays. Seems to me you might just as well admit to that. Beats the hell out of a capital charge."

He leaned over, his head dropping low between his legs, arms on his knees. The true sight of a beaten man. It didn't make me feel all that great. "You know what this will do to Blocker?" He looked up at me. "Do you have any idea? New York City's one thing, but a hick town like Tulsa?"

Now that offended me. Tulsa may not be all that big, but it had a gay community. Had to be at least three, four guys.

"Now that's true love, David. You're willing to put your neck on the block so that your boyfriend's reputation won't get smeared?"

He stood up and walked to the window. "That has nothing to do with it. How many people do you think will show up at his gallery for my exhibition if word gets out that Blocker Mays likes little boys?"

"Well, I would hope not a lot."

"You're a self-righteous prick."

I threw my hands up in the air. "What's the matter with you people? Whatever happened to screwing normal? Huh? We got us some sicko out there raping and murdering little old ladies, got you and Blocker messing with little boys! Jesus! Can't we find us a nice middle ground here?" I stood up. "Where were you? Just tell me, goddammit!"

"At Blocker's lake house. We have a witness. A teenage boy."

I looked heavenward and he said, "He was willing! Jesus, we paid him!"

"Well, that just makes everything real nice, now doesn't it?" I left.

On my way back to the station, I stopped by my half of Mrs. Horne's house and took a shower. Maybe it was the heat, or maybe it was David Perry's story. Whatever, I felt dirty.

I didn't know what to do with the information I had. So I called Detective Pruitt in Tulsa and told him he had a known pederast in his community. I got the impression that Detective Pruitt didn't like the idea a whole hell of a lot. I got the impression that maybe Blocker Mays might be moving real soon.

And then I called Laura and told her to keep Trent away from the neighbors.

"My God, Milt, are you serious? I've met David Perry, I just can't believe it."

"Well, believe it. It's true."

I could hear her shudder. "If he came anywhere near Trent—"

"He probably won't. Especially not now. But just to be on the safe side..."

"Of course. Oh, God, Milt, what is this world coming to?"

"You got me."

"Jerry's out of town. After what you told me, I sure could use some company tonight. Dinner?"

"Love to. What time?"

"Whenever you get free, just come on over."

"Okay, it's a date." And did that ever sound weird.

The kids were in bed and we sat in the windowed room and watched the dark take over the world. And we talked. She told me about her miscarriage between Rebecca and Adam and the subsequent hysterectomy immediately following Adam's birth. And how badly it all had affected her. And I told her about my marriage and my divorce, and, God forgive me, sometime that evening I told her about Glenda Sue.

"And you've felt guilty ever since, right?" she said, smiling kindly at me.

"Yeah. But I think I'm getting over that."

"You going to see her again?"

"Who? Glenda Sue?"

"Yes."

"No. Not that way, anyway. I think maybe now I can walk back into the Longbranch Inn without feeling like a leper, but that other part's all over."

"Why?"

Well, she had me there. What was I supposed to tell her? I wasn't going to sleep with Glenda Sue again because I was in love with another woman? I couldn't think about sleeping with anyone except another man's wife?

Finally, I shrugged and said, "I guess because I want more than just a roll in the hay."

She smiled. "You're a romantic, Milton Kovak."

"No crime against it, is there?"

"You'd know that better than I."

What I wanted to do was stand up, walk over to her, and pull her to her feet and kiss her. Instead, I stood up and walked to the door.

"It's getting late, Laura. I'd better be getting back. You and the kids gonna be okay?"

She smiled and stood up with me. "Yes, I'm not as scared as I pretended to be. I guess I just needed an excuse to get you over here."

We walked down the stairs together. "I thought we decided that friends didn't need to do that," I said.

At the door she touched my face lightly with the back of her hand. "Are we friends, Milt?" she asked softly.

I said, "Yeah," but I wasn't sure if she heard it. My throat was tight and the word came out in a strange-sounding croak. "I gotta go," I said and left.

On the drive back to Longbranch, I made up my mind about something. No more night visits to Laura's house. Only daytime visits. Only when the kids were up. Only when I couldn't touch her.

The world got back to normal, as normal as the world can get these days. The weeks passed and nothing much happened. Bill Williams had taken in the green Chevy and found out that it had been stolen out of Kansas City three months previously. What few prints showed up on it didn't match any in the files. So that was a dead end.

David Perry's house on Mountain Falls Road went up for sale, as did the gallery in Tulsa and the Mayses' home. Pruitt called to tell me that. He'd started pulling in Mays for every child-molestation case in the books, girls and boys, and Mays was ready to take it elsewhere. And I guess David was following.

We had one more rustling case toward the end of September, and lo and behold, we caught them in the act. It was an accident. Dalton Petigrew was driving out to his mama's house near Bulger and saw lights out in somebody's pasture. He thought maybe somebody had had a wreck and went out to help. Luckily, he remembered to pull his gun and hold it on them when he realized what was going on. We were able to tie the perps to all the other rustling cases in the area and we were pretty sure we had a case that was going to stick. I got a little flak about Dalton solving my case for me, but that was okay. At least that one was off the books.

The weeks passed. I went over to Laura's for lunch two or three times a week. After school started, we'd only had Adam as a chaperon, but I managed to remain a gentleman. Or a fool. Or whatever.

The first week in October we had another murder, but this one didn't have anything to do with Mrs. Munsky. This one was just the natural result of having a place like the Sidewinder in the county.

Now, we're not a dry county, so there's no law against having a place like the Sidewinder and I guess we should consider ourselves lucky that we only have the one. But that *one* has caused as much trouble as any three normal bars. It was out on Highway 5, north of Longbranch, and every redneck in a hundred-mile radius had to show up there sometime. We got calls on fights at the Sidewinder at least twice a week—fights over pool games, over gambling, over women, and just 'cause fighting is fun.

But that Friday night, the first week in October, I got called on my beeper because the fight had been with knives this time, and somebody was dead.

The somebody was Lloyd Bobber, and his dance partner had been Coy Henderson, who was sitting in a chair in the Sidewinder's big room with Dave the bartender standing over him with a baseball bat. And the reason was a Miss Angel Anne Crume.

When I walked in and saw Angel Anne sitting there with her legs crossed and looking at her manicure, I got plain mad. Angel Anne is one of these skinny girls with great bit tits, you know, the kind of girl who looks like she's on the verge of falling over all the time.

The first time I'd met Angel Anne was several years ago, when she was thirteen. I'd been called in by some neighbors because of the screams coming from Angel Anne's parents' house. The screams were actually coming from Angel Anne's mama, who was yelling at Angel Anne's daddy to stop trying to kill Angel Anne's brother Herbert. Seems Herbert and Angel Anne had been on intimate terms and Daddy had found out. So Daddy was going to kill Herbert. The only thing was, Herbert Crume is just about the stupidest boy I've ever met in my life and I figured if anybody had done any incestuous seducing, it wasn't him.

I had managed to get Mr. Crume off his son and get the boy to the hospital. When he finally got released, he up and joined the Navy, and as far as I know, hasn't been seen since. But Angel Anne, now that's a horse of a different color.

In the eight or nine years since that incident, there have been seventeen separate occasions when I or one of the other deputies has been called in to pull some dumb son of a bitch off some other dumb son of a bitch because of Angel Anne. She's not exactly the faithful type.

I suppose Angel Anne was the closest thing to a hooker we had in Longbranch. Though she would have denied the handle, saying she never did it for money. And I suppose she probably didn't. But she never paid a lick of rent, had a nice car that'd never cost her money, and her clothes were charged on somebody else's charge card.

I knew Angel Anne had been going with Coy Henderson for the past few weeks as steadily as she ever does. She'd been going the same way with Lloyd Bobber only a few months before. Even if Mrs. Bobber wasn't too keen on the idea. Well, witnesses said that Lloyd came in drunk and screaming that he was taking Angel Anne back. And Coy, drunk himself, said he wasn't. So the argument ended with a five-inch buck knife in a vital organ of Lloyd Bobber.

I took Coy in, went over and broke the news to the widow, then went back to the Sidewinder to talk with Angel Anne. One boyfriend was dead, one was in jail, and she was sitting on the lap of Earl Newhouse when I walked in. I took a skinny arm in my hand and led her to the back of the bar. If Prophecy County were a police state and I the ruler of the world, I'd have Angel Anne Crume deported to Texas. But as it stands now, being a democracy and all, there wasn't much I could do about Angel Anne.

I talked to her like a Dutch uncle for about fifteen minutes while she stared at her fingernails. When I'd finished, she said, "You know how much they charge for a manicure at Debbie's Cut and Curl? Five dollars! Don't that beat all!"

I left.

That weekend, it started getting cool for real. I got a call on my beeper on Monday night, and when I called the station, A.B. was on duty.

"Got a message for ya, Milt."

"Okay. Shoot."

"It's from that witness of yours, Mrs. Johnson?"

My stomach did one of those little flips it likes to do.

"Yeah?"

"She says to tell you it looks like rain? That mean anything to you?"

"That's just fine, A.B., thanks."

Looks like rain. Watching a storm come up in the windowed room. She'd called it erotic. I put on a jacket and got in the '55 and headed it out Highway 5 to Mountain Falls Road.

It was after eight o'clock when I got there. The kids were already in bed, but it was still a little light outside. Daylight saving time still had three weeks to go.

She smiled at me when she opened the door. "You said you always wanted to see a storm from that room."

"Yeah. I said that."

"Well, then, come on. There's a doozy brewing out there."

I didn't ask where her husband was. For one thing, she'd never invited me over when he was there before. For another, I didn't want to know. I figured if he was up in the windowed room waiting for us so we could all watch the storm together, I'd find some excuse to go on home. She took my hand and led me up the stairs to the windowed room. Black clouds hung over the twin peaks and you could see the rain falling on Tejas County. Lightning streaked the sky and soft sounds of thunder rumbled through the night. There was no light on in the room so that we could watch the storm build.

"I'm lucky. My kids sleep like the dead. And they're not afraid of thunderstorms. Lightning could strike the garage and I'd have to go get them out of bed. They'd never know it." She laughed softly.

The door was closed. We were alone in a dark room with a storm building up outside. And something building up inside, too.

I looked at her, silhouetted against the brighter light from the windows. She was wearing a loose sweater and jeans. I could see her nipples through the sweater. Her hair was down, brushing past her shoulders.

"Beautiful, isn't it?" she said, watching the sky.

"Yeah," I said, knowing what she meant but not looking at anything but her.

She turned and faced me. The thunder was getting louder and moving into closer sync with the lightning. Rain began making its little tapping sounds against the closed windows. We had been standing shoulder to shoulder. When she turned, we were standing face to face.

She lifted a hand and touched my face and I kissed her. Her mouth was hot and open and her arms went around my neck and her hands moved into my hair and my arms went around her waist and my hands found her ass and I pulled her tightly to me. When my mouth left hers, it found its way naturally to her neck and she let out a soft moan. When she did, I noticed it wasn't the first. I was moaning like an idiot. Somehow, clothes started flying. She had the most beautiful body I'd ever seen. There in the flickering lightning, like a light show in a bad movie, I looked at her and stroked her body and couldn't believe I was with her. She pulled me down on the floor on top of her.

Afterward, we lay together, naked, with the storm still going full swing. Somehow, I thought it would have been more poetic if the storm had ebbed as we did, but nature will only play along with you for so long.

She nestled her face in my neck and I stroked her fine back, feeling the little fuzz of hairs that grew at the small of her back.

"Oh, God, Milt," she said softly.

"Yeah."

"Oh, God."

I kissed her hair and her shoulder and felt her shudder. I stroked her back and my hand drifted down to her ass, what a fine ass, and I could feel her moving in a rhythmic way toward me. She began to kiss my throat and I felt one hand stroking my chest while the other, under me as we lay on the floor, began feeling its way down my back. I felt myself harden again. She removed her arm from under me and pushed me gently back so that I was lying on my back. She straddled me and lifted my hands to her breasts. Part of me figured maybe I was too old for two performances in such a short period of time, but the part of me that mattered didn't think so.

She moved above me like an apparition. The lightning lit up the sky and the thunder clapped and we moved together like a good rodeo rider and a bucking bronco. When she climaxed, I could feel it down to my toes. Her whole body shuddered and her cries could be heard above the thunder. I let go. How could anything in this world be better than making love to Laura Johnson?

I held her in my arms for hours on the cold floor of the windowed room. She cried for a little while, feeling those guilty feelings, and I held her and told her everything was going to be okay.

Finally, she said, "Milton?"

"What?"

"You think you can do it again?"

"What?"

"Well, if you don't, you'd better stop stroking me like that." She giggled.

I lay back on the floor, still holding on to her. "The mind is willing but the flesh is plumb tuckered out."

"Ummm," was all she said.

"Laura?"

"What?"

"I love—"

She put a finger to my lips. "Don't, Milt. Please." I could see the tears starting up in her eyes.

"But I do," I said.

She stroked my face with her hand and looked deep into my eyes. "I've never been with anyone like you," she said.

I laughed softly. "Is that good or bad?"

"Only the best."

I kissed her. Not the heated kind of kissing we'd been doing, but the kind of kiss that told her what she wouldn't let me say out loud.

"I guess I'm going to have to get out of here sometime," I said. "Wouldn't be good if the kids woke up."

"No, I guess not."

Off-key, I sang, "But baby, it's cold outside."

She laughed. "And hot in here."

"Very hot in here."

"Super-duper hot in here."

I pulled myself up and started searching for my clothes. "And if we wanna keep it from getting much hotter," I said, "then I'd better get the hell out of here."

We both dressed, me all the way, she in only sweater and her panties, and she walked me downstairs to the door. I held her for a long time at the closed door, trying not to think about the fact that she had on just those little flimsy silky lace panties. And that loose sweater that came off so easily.

"I gotta go," I said, still holding her.

"I know," she said, still holding me.

"Right now," I said, not letting go.

"Before we do something we'll both regret," she said in an ultradramatic voice, then giggled.

"You won't let me say it?" I asked, holding her away from me and looking into those incredible turquoise eyes.

She put a finger to my lips. "Get out of here, Milt, before we both say things that shouldn't be said."

That was enough for me.

TEN

THE NEXT MORNING I arrived at the station bright-eyed and bushy-tailed. Even though it had been a good deal after one in the morning when I'd arrived home, I had had the best night's sleep that I could remember. I was raring to go. Until I walked in the door and Gladys told me the sheriff wanted to see me right away because another old lady had gotten killed last night. Remember when you were a kid and your balloon got a slow leak in it? I think I must've looked something like that.

I went to the sheriff's office to get details I didn't want to hear.

"Happened in Mineola. So it's ours," he said. Mineola was up at the northern tip of Prophesy County, but it was still in Prophesy County. It was a nice little town about half the size of Longbranch, with a 2A football team that had made it to state three years in a row. The Mineola Bobcats would be missing one in their cheering section this year.

"An eighty-two-year-old grandmother of seventeen and great-grandmother of four. Same MO, far as we can tell."

"Nobody saw anything?" I asked just for the sake of asking.

"No."

"No tire marks or fingerprints?"

"No."

"Nothing?"

"Nothing."

The sheriff and I sat there and looked at each other and I figured I'd better do something pretty soon before I needed to start looking for another job. Because this one was going to play havoc come election time, whether Elberry Blankenship ran or not. The voters of Prophesy County don't take kindly to having their mamas and their grandmas butchered in their own homes. I wasn't taking too kindly to it myself.

I left the station and headed in my squad car to Mineola. It was a beautiful October morning, the sun was shining, and everything had been washed clean by the storm from the night before. The ride from Longbranch to Mineola went through lots of hills and timbered areas, across a few prairies where horses and cattle grazed, and gave me about forty-five minutes to think about Laura Johnson. I tried to remember feeling this way about the wife, and knew it had never been so. The passion had never been there. Not like last night. Not like Laura Johnson. Nothing in this world was like Laura Johnson. I had the car window open to feel the cool morning breeze, and the smells that came in the window—the scents of newly harvested fields, of a world washed clean—just reminded me of Laura Johnson.

As I turned into the driveway of the small frame house in the quiet residential area where the murdered woman had lived, I pushed thoughts of Laura out of my mind. Floyd Ackerman's hearse was just pulling out with the body when I arrived. Floyd had the county contract for ambulance work and his hearse doubled in that capacity. The fingerprint man was just closing up his case.

"Hey, Vernon," I said.

"Hey, Milt. How's it hanging?"

Which I thought was a sort of prophetic thing to ask on the day after a night like last night, but I just laughed.

"Anything?" I asked.

"Nada. The scum bucket don't leave shit. Ever."

"Yeah, he's a neat little bugger."

"See you later, Milt," he said and left, leaving me alone in the home of Mrs. Ida Worth, grandmother of seventeen and great-grandmother to four.

It reminded me of my mama's house, except with a lot more pictures. My mama only had the three grandchildren. It was a "shotgun" house, which is a house where you walk in the front door and there's a long hall going clean out the back, so if you fired a shotgun from the front door, the pellets would land in the backyard. The living room was on the right as you entered and the front bedroom was on the left, with the second bedroom connecting off it. The kitchen connected off the back of the living room. And that was that.

The furniture was a mixture of old and new, with some pieces that looked like somebody's ancestor had brought them over in a covered wagon, and some pieces that looked like they'd been bought at the K Mart. Mrs. Worth had been a crocheter, that was certain. There were doilies everywhere, on every conceivable surface and under every one of the much-prized pictures of the much-loved grandchildren, regulars and greats.

The only sign that something untoward had happened in this nice little house was a turned-over standing lamp with the bulb smashed to smithereens, and the blood. There wasn't much of that. In fact, I was surprised there was any. Our guy usually strangled his victims. I wondered why there was any blood at all. I started getting excited. Maybe she'd hurt him. Maybe we had a baddie out there with a bloody nose or a busted lip. Or maybe even better. Maybe we had a guy out there with a kitchen knife or sewing scissors in his ribs who'd have to go to the hospital. And if he went to a hospital, that would be just great. That would be fine.

I grabbed Mrs. Worth's phone and called the county hospital where Floyd Ackerman's hearse was taking the remains of the victim. As soon as I had the county coroner on the line, I asked, "Any blood on Mrs. Worth?"

"Yeah," Dr. Jim said. "She's got some slivers of glass in one arm, bleeding around the area. Why?"

Well, that was twice in one day I did my imitation of a balloon with a slow leak.

"Never mind," I said and hung up and sat down on Mrs. Worth's sofa and brooded over my plight in life. So the blood was Mrs. Worth's and not our fella's. But—if she'd bled enough from the broken light bulb to shed on the floor, maybe she'd shed on him too. So now what? Go look in every house, apartment, and trailer in Prophesy County and the surrounding areas for a man with blood on his sleeve? I was back to square one and I knew it. I didn't like it, but I knew it.

Somehow, it hardly seemed fair. Here I was, in love for the first time in my life, and I should be writing poems and smelling the clover, but instead I was in the house of an old lady who'd been violated beyond human comprehension, and wondering who, what, and where the animal that did it was, if you know what I mean. I was getting mad, which wasn't a half-bad idea. So far, I'd only been sad, and that hadn't got me very far. So I just sat there on the sofa and got good and mad, letting it boil up inside me and maybe bring out something, some little piece I knew but didn't know I knew, some little something, like in mystery books. But nothing came except a real, true anger that I didn't think I'd ever be able to shake.

There was a message from Laura when I got back. I called.

"Hey," I said.

"Hey yourself."

I'd closed the door to my office so nobody could hear my conversation, but I was still a little timid about it.

"How are you?" I asked, putting as much meaning into the words as possible.

"Fat and lazy, and sated."

She drew out the last word, making at least five syllables out of it.

I laughed. "Nothing fat on you, lady. I *know*. And as for lazy, well, I could testify to some energy, if you know what I mean."

She giggled and I laughed and I know we probably sounded like complete idiots.

"I woke up this morning," she said, "and I wanted you so much."

"Oh," I moaned into the phone. "Don't say that."

"Why?"

"'Cause I'll have to quit my job and come right over there and I can't afford it.''

"You got any vacation?''

"What?''

"You know, that free stuff they give you when you've been on a job awhile?''

"Yeah, I got some of that.''

"Then take it. About a week's worth. And come over here. We could make love while Adam's asleep, and when the kids get home from school, we could go places and do things...''

"Just so long as I leave before your husband gets home?''

That sobered us both up.

"Milt...''

"I'm sorry, baby. I shouldn't have said that. But I can't take any vacation anyway. We had another murder last night. Another old lady.''

She was silent for a minute and then she said, "That's awful. God, when is it gonna stop?''

"I wish I knew,'' I said.

"When can I see you again?'' she asked.

"It's up to you. I don't have anybody I have to hide us from.''

"Milt...''

"Sorry,'' I said again, "it just keeps coming out.''

"He won't be going out of town again until next week. We only have days until then.''

"Lunch? Tomorrow?'' It was already past noon now. It would have to be tomorrow.

"Tomorrow,'' she said and we both hung up and I felt alternately great and like a bagful of dog shit. Both. Over and over. Not a good sign.

And so I did everything I could do about Mrs. Worth, which wasn't much. I traced back all the incidents and tried to fit a pattern. There was none. I worked on some paperwork and went home to my empty nest with the new used sofa and drank a shit-pot full of light beer and thought about Laura.

The next morning I called all the other agencies with similar rape/strangulations and we talked. But nothing new came up. At noon, I left for Laura's.

She'd fed Adam an early lunch and he'd fallen asleep by the time I got there. I figured my time with Laura would be good for my diet because we didn't eat. Again, we went to the windowed room and shut the door and made love, twice, and, if anything, it was better than it had been the first time. It just kept getting better.

When I got back to the station I was an hour late, but nobody seemed to notice because nobody was there. Checking the log, I found out the day sergeant, Berle Mason, was out talking to the Longbranch High School senior class about a career in law enforcement, Mike was at the scene of a car wreck on Lowell Road up near Tejas County, Dalton was talking to the victims of a burglary out in Bishop, and the sheriff, seeing as I wasn't around, had gone to answer a silent alarm at Hyden's Feed and Grain over in Mineola. While I was reading the log, Gladys came back into the room.

"Where you been, Milt?" she asked.

"Had some personal business to take care of," I said, not blushing. I was beginning to get good at this.

"Well, the sheriff was PO'd when he had to take that call. You better brace yourself for when he gets back."

"Yeah," I said and left her standing there looking at me the way the wife used to look at me when I farted in the living room.

I went into my office and looked at my desk and didn't like what I saw. Too much stuff on it and none of it doing me a bit of good. I sat down and decided to organize, which isn't one of my strong points. I had seven little piles going when Gladys opened my office door without knocking first, which wasn't like her. I looked up and didn't like what I saw. Our always-staid Gladys was white as a sheet, the face powder standing out like talcum on a baby's butt.

"Milton," she said.

"Gladys? What's wrong?"

I stood up and walked to the doorway where she stood leaning against the jamb for support.

"It's the sheriff," she said in a strange new voice. "He's been shot."

"Where is he?"

"He's being transported to County Memorial now."

I was out of the station like a shot, excuse the expression, and on my way to the hospital.

Now don't think for a minute that I dwelled too long on the fact that the sheriff took a bullet that should have been mine. Don't think that I even considered the fact that if I hadn't been screwing somebody else's wife, the sheriff would be in his office at that very minute doing business as usual. You don't think about that, and I won't think about that. Deal?

I got to the hospital with my siren going full blast and pulled up to the emergency-room entrance. I think I may have left the door of the squad car open in my rush for the emergency-room doors, but I don't really remember. When I finally got through all the questions and to the right person to tell me the answer, I found out the sheriff was still in surgery. I also found out that one boy was dead and one critically wounded. Two Mineola Bobcats playing cops and robbers for real. It wasn't a real good year for the people of Mineola.

I called Gladys and told her where I was and that the sheriff was still in surgery and I didn't know anything at this point. She said she'd get Dalton in from Bishop and notify Mike to finish up as quick as he could on the wreck and get back in, and notify Berle at the high school. I also told her to call A.B., Jasmine, and Alton, our regular night shift, inform them of the situation, and have them on stand-by status. She said, "Will do," and I wondered how come we were both talking militarese, but I didn't wonder for long because I had other things on my mind.

I left the hospital to go to the sheriff's house. Nadine Blankenship is a nice lady in her late fifties, pretty in a used-to-be sort of way. Round and pink and kind of soft looking. The kind of lady who bakes cookies and goes to rummage sales. But she was also a mean poker player and no-nonsense mother. I'd have rather made myself a human sacrifice than walk into her neat little house and tell her where her husband was. But I had a job, and sometimes, when I'm not out screwing married women, I do it.

Cops' wives, and husbands, I suppose, too, come in two different flavors. The kind that can't handle it, like my wife, and the kind that can, like Nadine Blankenship. When I told her her husband had been shot, she asked two questions:

"Is he dead?"

"No, ma'am."

"Where is he?"

"At County Memorial."

And we went together. She didn't shed a tear and she didn't say a word. Most of all, she didn't say "Why was he out on a call when you should have been?" She didn't say that and I was grateful.

We sat together in the waiting room outside the surgery for two hours. The first hour, she called both her kids, the boy in college at Norman, and the girl living with her husband in Oklahoma City, and told them. They were both on their way down. Then she called Mrs. Horne, my landlady and the sheriff's mama's cousin, and asked her to go over to Mrs. Blankenship's house and sit with her. And that she'd call there soon as she had any news.

Mike came by in the first hour but just for moral support. He was unusually quiet for Mike. I noticed right off the bat that he didn't say, "Why was the sheriff out on a call when you should have been?"

When Dalton came by twenty minutes after Mike left, he didn't say it either. But I knew everybody was thinking it.

The second hour, Mrs. Blankenship started talking. She told me about her courtship and marriage, and went into details of her wedding night, details I've since conveniently forgotten. She told me of the births of both of her children, right here in County Memorial, and how bad the second one, the boy, had been. How it had ripped something they couldn't fix and she'd had to have a hysterectomy. I thought fleetingly of Laura, but pushed it out of my mind as quickly as possible.

She told me how hard she had worked in her husband's first and only campaign for the office of sheriff. She told me about Elberry's father dying of cancer in this very hospital and how Elberry had cried. She gave me the recipe for her mother's cornmeal muffins, which was a family secret. She told me about the time she had found a baggie of marijuana in Elberry Jr.'s dresser drawer and how she had never told the sheriff about it but had dealt with it herself by having the boy become a weekend volunteer in the emergency room of this very hospital.

After two hours, the doctor came out of the operating room and told us that Elberry Blankenship was going to live. The bullet had lodged itself close enough to the heart to scare the hell out of the surgeons, but they had been able to remove it without damage to any vital organs. The doctor said that the sheriff would be able to leave the hospital in a few days, and with a few weeks rest at home he'd be fine.

Mrs. Blankenship turned to me and said, "Milton, I'd appreciate it if you'd forget everything I just told you. And if you ever give anyone my mother's recipe for cornmeal muffins, I'll rip off your head and tell God you died."

I smiled and said, "Yes, ma'am."

ELEVEN

Now, GETTING SHOT, I hear, is not one of the world's greatest pleasures, and even with the prognosis being good, the sheriff was still going to be in bed for a couple of weeks. I didn't envy Mrs. Blankenship trying to keep him there, either.

As punishment for not being where I was supposed to be when I was supposed to be, the sheriff put me in charge. The first thing I did as acting sheriff was call Mrs. Laura Johnson and tell her I wouldn't be able to sleep with her in the daytime anymore.

Guilt's a funny little puppy, you know? I discovered somewhere along the way that I was blaming Laura for the sheriff being shot, rather than accepting the fact that, as deputies go, I was dog shit.

Later that night, the boy that didn't die regained consciousness. So I went to talk a little with him. Now, I knew this boy's daddy. I'd been two years ahead of him in high school and he hadn't been a bad sort. And I knew that this boy, Jason Smith, was supposed to be a good kid. Co-captain of the Mineola Bobcats, vice president of his senior class, and a member of Mineola's Honor Society, with a straight B average. The boy that had died wasn't much different. They were good boys from good families who just happened to decide one day to rob the Hyden's Feed and Grain and shoot the sheriff of Prophesy County while they were about it. I wanted to know why. That's the kind of acting sheriff I am.

And that's when I discovered that we had a crime wave with a capital C in Prophesy County. Not only did we have murderers and rapists and rustlers and convenience-store robbers, but we had us a "Fagin," if you'll excuse the literary reference, to deal with.

His name in this incarnation, according to Jason Smith, was Bobby. No last name. Just Bobby. It took about three hours of interrogation to get the facts out of the boy, but they went something like this.

Three months before, Jason and his best friend, Justice Laws (his daddy had a sense of humor but I guess he wasn't laughing now), had skipped school on Justice's birthday. And they'd gone joy-riding in Jason's mama's Buick while she was at a Ladies' Auxiliary meeting. Somewhere in Tejas County, they'd picked up a hitchhiker named Bobby. Who had on him three marijuana cigarettes dusted with what they call angel dust.

Now Bobby, according to Jason, was a grown man, somewhere in his late twenties, and in the short time they had known him, he always had a lot of money and a lot of dope. Just for the hell of it, I asked Jason if this Bobby had stringy blond hair and ever drove a green Chevy. Unfortunately, Bobby was of the black persuasion.

Now Jason says he didn't do any of it, but that Justice started playing with what they call crack, which is some kind of nasty shit they make out of cocaine, the way I understand it. And Bobby seemed to have a lot of that, at first. And then he didn't. He didn't have any, and Justice was not doing too well, according to Jason.

And Bobby told Justice that if he'd liberate his daddy's cash register at his daddy's dry-cleaning shop, then the crack would magically appear. Which he did and it did, if you know what I mean.

And then, of course, a few days later, the crack dried up again and it seemed like the only way to make it magically appear again was to hit a certain gas station out on Highway 5. Which Justice did with Jason's help. And on and on until they had orders to hit the Hyden's Food and Grain, where the whole thing just sort of blew up in their faces, if you know what I mean.

I swear to God, sometimes I think kids are even dumber than I give 'em credit for. So now, the order of the day was to find Bobby. Which I doubted we would, because as soon as the first shot was fired I figured Bobby was headed for Dallas. Or somewhere.

Which got me to thinking about men. I figure you got three types. First, you got the hunters, whether they're hunting rabbits, real estate, or poontang. They go out in search of their prey, sneak up on its blind side, and dismember it. Second, you got your fishers. They're the slow, methodical type. They talk soft and carry a big stick, but the results are basically the same. Something that once was whole no longer is. Thirdly, you got your couch potatoes. In which category I place myself. They're the type that lie around with a wounded expression on their faces and let the world come to them, or, preferably, just let it pass on by. Which doesn't mean diddly-squat, except that

Prophecy County seemed to be filling up with hunters, and deer season was still two weeks off.

But these hunters weren't looking for deer. They were looking for little old ladies, small boys, and teenagers. I figured it was time this couch potato got off his butt and started hunting the hunters.

I stayed at the station all the rest of the week trying to figure out what was on the sheriff's desk. On Monday night, Laura called me.

"Milt? Are you coming over tonight?"

Which meant that her husband had gone out of town like she'd said he would. As mad as I was at her and at me, it didn't take two seconds to say yes.

But before I had a chance to change my clothes in my half of Mrs. Horne's house, I got a call from Jasmine, who was on duty that night.

"Milt?"

"Hey."

"You got a call from Haywood Hunter. Out at Falls End?"

"Yeah? What he want?"

She sighed. It was a sad sigh. "He wouldn't say. Just wants you to call him." And she hung up.

So I called Haywood.

"This is Milt, Haywood. You wanted me?"

"I hear you're acting sheriff now?" he said.

"That's what they tell me."

"Then why don't you come on out here an act like a sheriff?" he said and laughed like an idiot.

"What's up?"

"Well, I got me this kid been sitting up at the top of the Falls for two days now."

"What?"

"This kid. Don't know him. About seventeen, I'd guess. Got about a hundred six-packs with him, I figure, the way he's been throwing the cans around. He's just sitting up there ass-deep in the water, singing sad songs. I'm not kidding you, Milt. God's truth."

"Well, tell him to leave."

"I've been telling him! He won't! Says he's gonna jump. Just soon as he drinks up the beer."

"Shit."

"My sentiments exactly. I don't got anybody at the camp now, so he's not bothering anybody but me, but still, what am I supposed to do if this little fuck-up decides to do it? Put him in a Hefty bag and leave him for the trash?"

"No. Don't seem right somehow, Haywood. I'll be along in a minute."

So I finished getting dressed up for Laura's and swung on by Haywood's first, and sure enough, there was this kid up at the top of the Falls, which is at the back of Mrs. Munsky's farm, just sitting there drunk as you please singing some sad song I'd heard on the radio by that new singer, some pretty black lady named Houston.

I climbed up the least steep side of the mountain, snagging my new jacket I'd bought to impress Laura and getting mud on my shoes.

The kid didn't have a half-bad voice. "Didn't we almost have it all?" he sang sad and sweet and then belched. I moved over beside him to sit on the bank of Jennifer Creek. He was sitting in the middle, with the water swishing around him and going over his legs and down the Falls. He looked over at me and silently offered me a beer.

"Thank you kindly, son," I said, taking the offered beer and popping the top. It wasn't a light either. God gives us these little blessings at the strangest times. "Sure is pretty up here," I said.

He nodded his head and sniffed. Tears were running down his cheeks.

"But it's gonna get mighty cold tonight. Heard that on Channel 3. Supposed to get down to the mid-fifties. Gonna be awful damn cold in that water."

He didn't respond at all. Just sat there, too damn close to the edge for me to grab him. And then he started singing again. The same song. Sad song when you think about it. Almost having it all. But not quite. Real sad.

"What's your name?" I asked when he stopped singing to take a swig of his beer. Again there was no response. "I'm Milt. Milt Kovak." I stretched out a hand as if to shake but he just looked at it. He was just drunk, not stupid. "Surely do wish we could go on down there to Falls End and sit around Haywood's fire and talk a little bit. Then, if you still wanna come on up here, well, who am I to stop you?"

The kid was the real quiet type. So I said, "You wanna tell me about her? Your girl?"

He sobbed in some night air and stared out at the darkening world. "She ain't my girl anymore." Well, that was something, I figured. A line of communication, so to speak.

"You two have a little spat?"

He shook his head. "No. She just doesn't wanna see me anymore. Ever again." He looked over at me and the whites of his eyes were shinning from the reflection of the newly risen moon. They shone like something not quite real.

I smiled. "She'll get over it, boy. Hell, they always do. They say that all the damn time. You just gotta bend like the willow. I bet if you called her right now from Haywood's store, she'd be crying 'cause she hasn't seen you in two days. Wondering where you been. I'd bet a million dollars I'm right."

He was studying me real close. Listening hard to everything I said. "You really think so?" he asked.

"You betcha."

And nice as you please, he got up, staggering a little so I had to grab him so he wouldn't go over the Falls now that he decided maybe life was worth living, and we walked on down to Haywood's.

Haywood got a blanket and we wrapped the boy up but he wasn't interested in that. He wanted the phone. So we let him make his call.

"Dorothy? It's me. Honey . . ."

And the little darling hung up in his face. And the boy headed for the door. It took all my strength and all Haywood's to get him down and it was a constant battle until Floyd Ackerman's hearse got there to take him to the hospital. I wasn't going to haul him in now, or after the doctors released him. I hoped that once he sobered up, he'd forget about jumping. But I called Jasmine at the station and told her to get over to the hospital, find out who the boy was, and contact his parents.

And then I reflected a little while on what we so-called humans do to each other and ourselves. I figured God giving us a brain was a two-sided coin. It made us smart enough to get to the moon and back and dumb enough to fall in love. I cleaned up as best I could and headed up the mountain to Laura's.

The kids were asleep by the time I got there. I'd sort of wanted to see them but then we ended up in the windowed room upstairs and I forgot about them completely. Afterward, we lay together under an afghan and held each other. And I did something real stupid.

"I want you to marry me," I said.

She turned and looked at me with those turquoise eyes bigger than I'd ever seen them. "Is this a joke?"

"I'm not laughing."

"In case you haven't notice, Milt, I already am. Married, I mean."

I sat up and pulled on my T-shirt and stared out the windows. "You're married, but you don't have a husband and your kids don't have a daddy. You know that and I know that. Like you said, you just got you another kid. If you want four kids instead of three, marry me and we'll adopt one of our own."

She sat up too and I could feel her eyes on the back of my neck. "My God, you're serious."

I turned to face her and I kissed her lips hard. "Yeah, I'm goddamn serious, lady."

She pulled away and stood up, her naked body paler than ever in the moonlight. She walked over to where her clothes rested in a heap and started putting them on.

"You want me, Milt. But you don't need me. Jerry needs me."

"Goddammit, I do need you. Maybe not to wipe my butt like Jerry does, but I need you!"

"Stop it!"

She turned to face me and tears were rolling down her cheeks and she wasn't beautiful for a minute. She was just a woman in agony.

"Don't talk about him. He's my husband! He's the father of my children! Don't you ever breathe his name again, you hear me?"

I got dressed and left, feeling worse than I'd ever felt in my life. Feeling like a kid whose dog just died. Feeling like a man who just hurt the woman he loved. Feeling like homemade shit.

And the next day I found out that Mrs. Bertha Hoffsteader, age seventy-three, had been killed in her home in Lydecker in Tejas County. Bill Williams reported to me on the phone that there were no prints, no tire tracks, no clues, and no semen.

By this point, our polite rapist was making the news in Tulsa and Oklahoma City. He was in the newspapers and on the TV and some jerked-off state legislator was calling for a reform of the county sheriff system of the whole state. Like that would do a whole hell of a lot of good. Goddamn politicians. I got a call that afternoon from the sheriff.

"You gonna sit there and cost me my job, Milt, or you gonna go out and get me that goddamn asshole?" he asked in his friendly sort of way.

I was not what you'd call a happy man at the moment, so I said, "You wanna tell me exactly how to go about doing that, Elberry? You tell me, and I'll go do it. No problem."

"Don't get smart with me, boy. I can still fire your ass even if I'm laying on mine, you understand?"

I sighed. "Sheriff, the one thing in this world I'd like to do more than any other is find me that goddamn rapist. You wanna know the truth, he scares the shit out of me. He really does. I keep thinking about Mrs. Horne, and your mama—"

"You leave my mama out of this."

"And every other old lady in this county, and I get scared and I get mad. But that don't get me the guy."

"You figure out any pattern? What's the dates on these?"

So I told him. The first one we knew about was in Lauden, in Tabor County, on April 12. Then nothing until June 7 in the country in Tejas County. Then Bulger in Tabor County again on July 5, then again in Tejas County on July 25. Mrs. Munsky was on August 15, the best we can figure, and then again a week later in Tejas County, on August 22. Ida Worth wasn't until October 10. And one week later, Mrs. Bertha Hoffsteader.

"Get your butt over to my house," the sheriff said and hung up.

So I got my butt over to his house. The sheriff lived in a neighborhood of Longbranch that had been new in 1952. There'd been a rumor about the Army building a base in Longbranch and some developer had counted his chickens a bit early and built twenty-three houses on spec. The base never became a reality, the developer went belly up, but the twenty-three houses got sold eventually.

Originally, they'd all looked alike, as housing developments do, little ticky-tacky houses all in a row, but some people had planted pecan trees and some elm trees, some had added screened-in porches and some had turned their garages into dens. Some had added carports and one industrious individual had even added a second story. Now Mistletoe Avenue was a nice little street bustling with kids and barbecuing parents, and no two houses looked alike.

The original three-bedroom, one-bath, one-car-garage house that the newlyweds Elberry and Nadine Blankenship had bought was now a four-bedroom, one-bath and one *California* bath, den, and carport house. The sheriff was in the master bedroom. Beside the bed was a child's blackboard attached to a small rolling desk. The draperies were pulled across the sliding glass doors that I knew looked out on the covered patio and gas grill.

"Lookee here," the sheriff said, pointing at the blackboard. On it, in his cramped handwriting, were three columns. They looked something like this:

Mrs. Coreen Middleburg	Lauden, Tabor Co. (8 weeks)	4/12
Miss Irene Brown	Tejas County (4 weeks)	6/7
Mrs. LaVerne Price	Bulger, Tabor Co. (20 days)	7/05
Mrs. Alnetta Bulle	Tejas County (3 weeks)	7/25
Mrs. Beatrice Munsky	Prophesy County (1 week)	8/15
Mrs. Agnes Smithfield	Tejas County (7 weeks)	8/22
Mrs. Ida Worth	Mineola, Prophesy Co. (1 week)	10/10
Mrs. Bertha Hoffsteader	Lydecker, Tejas Co.	10/17

"You notice anything?" the Sheriff asked me.

"You mean other than there's too goddamn many of 'em?"

"You notice these last five?" he asked, pointing. "They all happened on the same day of the week. Namely, Monday. And you see these first three? They all happened on a Tuesday."

"Uh-huh," I said, trying to sound like I knew what it all meant. I didn't say "So what?" but I was thinking it.

I tried not to notice the slight whine in his voice when he said, "Well, Milt, it's *something*. The only pattern of any kind that we got. We got us two big bunches of time when nothing happened. Namely between the first and the second and between Mrs. Smithfield and Mrs. Worth. But even those in the middle aren't consistent. Why's that, Milt?"

"I dunno, Sheriff."

"Could be a lot of reasons, Milt. Could be maybe he was out of town on business? Maybe we got some rape/strangulation cases as far away as Denver, Houston, I dunno, connected to this? Or maybe he didn't do nothing during these times. Maybe he had his demons under control for a little while. I don't give a damn, personally."

I looked at the blackboard. Mondays—the last five had been on Mondays. The first three on Tuesdays. Interesting.

"So what's he got on Monday nights and Tuesday nights that's different than Wednesday nights or Thursday nights, Sheriff?" I asked.

"Good question. Maybe his mama goes bowling on Monday nights. Or his wife or roommate or whatever. Maybe she used to go on Tuesday, but they changed it to Monday. Or something like that." He looked at me in a desperate sort of way. I'd never seen the sheriff like this and I figured it had as much to do with wanting to keep his hand in as finding out who killed those ladies. Maybe that wasn't very charitable of me, but there it is.

Mrs. Blankenship came in with a TV tray with glasses of iced tea and some chips in a bowl. She set it down in front of the sheriff, scowled at me, and left without a word. But her meaning had been clear enough. Don't stay too long, don't say anything to upset him, and don't punch him in the stomach. I got the message.

Now I've already given you my own personal breakdown on the kinds of men in this world. Now let me give you my breakdown on women. There is none. Women are probably what God meant to make when he made Adam and screwed it up. They are *diversified.* None two alike. Like amoebas or snowflakes.

You think you may have them pegged, like the sweet little lady who sits around and knits and wouldn't swat a fly. Then you mess with her man or one of her kids and she cuts off your balls and hands 'em to you.

Or you take your liberated woman, female yuppie variety, who's into job, the proper places to eat, and voting for the right person. Then you look in the bottom-right-hand drawer of her bureau, way behind the lace undies, maybe hidden in the toe of a crew sock (color-coordinated to match her running shoes), and you'll find pictures of Mama and Daddy and a little girl in pigtails.

You take my wife (I'm not Henny Youngman, so don't expect me to say please). Sweetest little thing in the world. Soft and virginal and hardly ever opened her mouth. A year after I married her I was asking permission to piss.

No, you can't pigeonhole women. But if I knew anything in this world about them, I knew I wasn't about to mess with Mrs. Nadine Blankenship or her man. Not if I didn't want to talk soprano the rest of my life.

I finished up with the sheriff, telling him in as un-condescending a manner as possible that he done good, then left to go back to being acting sheriff at the station. A job that included a daily report by Berle Mason as to the quantity and quality of his day. Which was as boring as you'd expect. I left the station at six and went home to my half of Mrs. Horne's house.

As I popped the top of my first light of the day, the phone rang.

"Milton Kovak," I said.

"Mr. Kovak?" came a high, squeaky, but male voice. "This is Burgess Talbott from the church."

I didn't know any Burgess Talbott and I wasn't sure which church.

"Yes?"

"Mrs. Horne told me you might be interested in joining the choir? We sure could use a tenor or two up there come Sunday morning?"

"Oh. Well. I haven't thought about it, actually, Mr. Talbott."

"Mrs. Horne said we should call you? Said you had a fine voice?"

I wondered when Mrs. Horne had ever heard me sing. The wife always said I sounded like a moose in heat. But come to think of it, the choir at Mrs.

Horne's church sounded a lot like a bunch of tomcats fighting over a dead fish. If that was their ultimate goal, I might be a help.

"Well, Mr. Talbott, I'm a little busy now, I'm acting sheriff—"

"Choir practice is on Wednesday nights? Just an hour? Then you come to church on Sunday? Not too much time, what do you think, Mr. Kovak?"

"Well..."

"It sure would help the church? And we'd be mighty grateful?"

"Choir practice tomorrow night?"

"At seven o'clock? Can we expect you?"

I sighed. It was something to do. "Sure, Mr. Talbott, I'll be there with bells on."

"Thank you, Mr. Kovak." And we said good-bye. And I sat down on the sofa and finished my beer, thinking the First Baptist Church of Longbranch, Oklahoma, was in for one hell of a treat.

TWELVE

WEDNESDAY WAS business as usual at the station. Dalton was out on a two-car head-on collision on Highway 5 where it meets FM 312, one carful of teenagers skipping school and one old, half-blind farmer. So far we had two girls dead, three boys in critical condition, and a very confused farmer.

I had Mike go over to Tejas County and coordinate our information with Bill Williams, and Berle was out at the County Home Ec office speaking to a group of old ladies about how the Sheriff's Department was there to help them and what they should do about the current rapist/murderer in our midst.

That evening I found a package about two feet tall, three feet wide, and about an inch thick on the little porch of my half of Mrs. Horne's house. I picked it up, opened the door and went in. Once I had my beer in my hand I opened the package. It was a picture of two people, a man and a woman, in silhouette, standing close together with their arms around each other, staring out a window at some pretty scenery. Underneath, it had a date and the name of a gallery and the artist's name. Taped to the glass was a note.

"I'm sorry. Laura."

I picked up the phone and dialed, but when a man answered, I asked for John Smith and was told I had the wrong number. I hung up.

And I sat down and held the picture and looked at it and thought about Laura. Beautiful Laura. Then I thought about the man's voice who'd answered the phone and realized I had no idea what her husband even looked like. And I guessed that I probably didn't want to know.

I remember after my second beer that I was supposed to go to choir practice that night, so I went in the bathroom and brushed my teeth and used some mouthwash I found in the cabinet. Must have gotten there by mistake when the wife and I were splitting up the contents of our lives. I squished the mouthwash around in my mouth, thinking how much it tasted like bad booze, spit it out and got dressed to go to choir practice. I didn't know what you were supposed to wear on such an occasion, so I chose a pair of chino pants, a blue button-down-collar shirt, and my red windbreaker with "Oklahoma Sooners" written on the back.

The church was only three blocks from Mrs. Horne's house so I decided to walk. It was a great October evening, cool enough to be interesting, and the crunch of newly fallen leaves under my feet made a nice friendly sound. It was just beginning to get dark as I turned the corner where the church stood. I saw lights on in the Sunday-school wing and went in that direction.

I recognized Burgess Talbott when he came up and shook my hand as the man that led the choir every Sunday. There were three people I knew by name in the choir, and four I knew by sight. They were friendly and not one of them sang any better than I did. I had a great time.

Afterward, I walked home with a lady named Mrs. Richards, who lived on the block behind Mrs. Horne. She was the lead soprano with a cracking voice and high notes that sounded like fingernails on a blackboard. I walked the block out of my way to see her safely to her door and gave her my standard speech about not letting anybody in her house and where to find me if she needed me.

She was sweet about it but said, "I'm ninety years old, Mr. Kovak. If it's my time, it's my time. God will let me know. And if he chooses to take me home in such a way, then there's a reason neither you nor I know about. But thank you anyway."

I walked on home thinking about Mrs. Munsky and Mrs. Worth and wondering if it had been God's will that they went home in such a way. Somehow, I doubted it. Mrs. Richards and I must not be talking about the same God. The one I knew about didn't truck with men that killed and raped and hurt. I thought it might be interesting to get into a good philosophical discussion someday with Mrs. Richards.

I went into my apartment and sat down on the sofa without a beer and started thinking about Mrs. Munsky and how she must have been when LeRoy was a little boy. How she must have scolded him when he was bad and hugged him when he was good, and how she must have blushed a little when her husband got frisky, and how good her fried chicken must have been. And I thought about Ida Worth and her seventeen grandchildren and four great-grandchildren and how she much have opened her arms wide to take in that many, and I could see them sitting around the kitchen of that little shotgun house eating cookies and drinking milk and asking Grandma why the sky was blue. And my heart ached. And it took a lot not to call Mrs. Richards up on the phone and tell her how wrong she was.

The next day I was notified by Emmett Hopkins, chief of police of Longbranch, that Mrs. Bradley (Nora) Limone had been raped and strangled in her home on Summit Avenue sometime during the night. Emmett asked me if I'd mind looking at the scene. I minded a lot but I went anyway. I took the county coroner with me.

Mrs. Bradley Limone lived on Summit Avenue in a big old house as close to a mansion as you can get in Longbranch. It was three stories tall and had a lot of gewgaws on the porch, Victorian style. And Mrs. Bradley Limone hadn't lived alone, as all the other victims had. She'd lived with a full-time nurse, her daughter Amanda, and Amanda's husband, Luther Babcock, and their two children, a girl of ten and a boy of fourteen.

In questioning Mrs. Babcock, we found out that last night had been the nurse's night off, that she and her children had gone to a movie, and that her husband had been out playing poker with some friends. She'd looked in on her mother when she got home, but everything had looked fine. The old lady had looked as if she were asleep. It wasn't until in the morning, by the light of day, that the nurse saw what had happened.

In examining the body, Dr. Jim offered another discrepancy. "Milton, come look at this," he said.

I walked carefully over to the bed where the old lady lay.

"Lookee here, Milton. There's semen all over the damn place," he said.

I said, "Mighty interesting," or something to that effect, and walked back over to the door where the police chief stood. After a quick look, Dr. Jim shook his head and joined us.

"Either our guy's getting weirder than ever, Milton, or we got us a copycat here," he said.

"Why you say that, Dr. Jim?" I asked.

"Because this lady's been violated all right, but not with a penis. Looks like somebody stuck a broom handle up her after she was already dead. And all that semen looks like somebody jerked off. There's none inside the vagina, all of it's just around the top of her and on the sheets." He shook his head. "This is plumb sick, Milton. I mean it."

Emmett and I left and let the medicos do their thing. We went out to the driveway and sat in his squad car.

"We never told anybody 'bout the fact there's never any semen around, Emmett, and I'd be obliged if you didn't say anything," I told him.

"Yeah. You got it. But, Milton..."

"What you think old Luther Babcock was doing last night? You really think he was playing poker?"

Emmett shook his head back and forth. "Jesus, Milton..."

"I know, Emmett. Saying a guy done this to his own mother-in-law is almost as sick as doing it, but..."

"She was loaded. Old man Limone must have left over a million when he died. And that's in cash. No telling how much in land and such."

"Which'll all probably go to Amanda with her mama dead?"

"More 'n likely."

We sat there in silence for a while, both thinking some pretty nasty things.

Finally, Emmett sighed and looked at me as she opened his car door. "Well, I best go talk to Luther and find out who he was supposed to be playing with last night and talk to 'em. See if his alibi sticks."

I nodded as he got out but stayed where I was, deep in my own nasty thoughts. I didn't envy Emmett his job. Either he was going to have to accuse an innocent man of doing unspeakable things to his mother-in-law, or he was going to have to arrest him for doing it, and listen to the howls of the betrayed wife and daughter. I got out of the police chief's car and walked over to my own and drove on back to the station.

And thought about Laura all the way there. So much nicer a thing to think about than Luther Babcock and his mother-in-law. I thought about how Laura felt and tasted and smelled, how she smiled and frowned and laughed, and then I thought about the last thing she'd said to me. "Don't even breathe his name to me." I had no rights. Not to talk about us or them. I was in over my head and I was beginning to realize it, but that didn't keep me from wondering if she was busy at lunch today. Or keep me from calling her the minute I was behind the closed doors of the sheriff's office.

"I thought you said you couldn't come over during the daytime?" she said when I had her on the phone.

"Yeah. I said that."

"Well?"

"I want to see you."

"I want to see you too."

And that was all she wrote. I got in the squad car and headed south on Highway 5 to Mountain Falls Road. Out of beeper range. Out of my mind.

Adam was awake when I got there, busily eating a mushed-up cookie grasped firmly in his pudgy, slimy little hand. He and I talked for a few minutes, with only him totally understanding the conversation. He seemed very pleased with what we both said.

She was in a baggy pair of jeans and a chambray workshirt big enough to be a man's. It didn't bear thinking about what man had originally worn it. She wore no makeup and her feet were clad in crew socks. And she was so beautiful it made my heart hurt just to look at her. She passed by me as I sat at the picnic table with Adam and touched my hair lightly with her hand. A shiver went up and down my spine and my palms began to sweat. I figured if this was what love was all about, the songs had it all wrong. This wasn't lollipops and roses, this was pure hell.

After Adam had mangled the last of his chocolate-chip cookie, I held him down while Laura washed him off and we laughed at his faces and statements, which Laura translated for me. Something to the effect that he was saving that last piece of cookie under his left ear for after his nap. Then she took him upstairs and I followed. I sang him a song I had learned at choir practice the night before and Laura did a credible job of not laughing out loud at my voice. As his eyelids began to close, she and I tiptoed out of his room and made our way to the windowed room and managed to get most of our clothes off before we hit the floor.

As I got back into beeper range, the damned thing went off and I made it to a gas station on the highway to call the station.

"Where you been?" Gladys asked.

"Personal business. What's up?" I was a little abrupt but I figured as acting sheriff I didn't need to explain my whereabouts to anyone. Of course, if I'd been at the dentist, I would have told her.

"Where are you?"

"On Highway 5 at Clyde's Texaco."

"Good. You're the closest. There's a wreck out your way. 'Bout five minutes further into town. You handle it?"

"Sure," I said and hung up. Nothing makes an afternoon like seeing dead, burned bodies.

But I was lucky. And so were the occupants of the two vehicles involved. It was more than a fender bender, but no fatalities. A possible broken nose in one car and a torn ear in another. But if I hadn't gotten there when I did, things might have gotten worse.

"You stupid dumb-ass hick!" was what I heard as I got out of the squad car. The spokesman was an obvious salesman type on his way through our county to somewhere where they bought his widgets, or whatever. His three-martini lunch smelled all over the place.

The stupid, dumb-ass hick, namely Brett Blodgett of Bishop, who was a lawyer, took offense to the salesman's name-calling and shoved him. Not the smartest thing for a lawyer to do, but he was bleeding. Seeing their own blood tends to make some people a mite fidgety.

"You goddamn Yankee asshole" was Brett's reply as he shoved, and the Yankee asshole, whose accent sounded more like he came from Dallas, took offense and shoved back, holding his ripped and bleeding ear with one hand.

I did what acting sheriffs do so well and defused the situation, mainly by telling them that if they didn't cut it out, they'd be bleeding all over the county lockup. As the salesman wouldn't be able to see his widgets from the lockup, and Brett realized the embarrassment and scandal of such an event to his position in the community, they cut it out.

But I had to take the salesman in anyway because he was drunk as a skunk. Brett handed the drunk his card as he pulled away. I swear to God, lawyers kill me.

After I got the salesman all cozy in the lockup, I went into the sheriff's office and called Emmett.

"Hey, Milt," he said after I identified myself. His voice sounded bad. It sounded like the voice of a man who'd seen and heard a little too much in his lifetime. Sometimes, I recognized that voice coming out of me.

"You talk to Luther?" I asked.

"Yeah. And I talked to the boys he was with last night. He was playing poker all right."

"All night? Never left?"

"Well, that's the problem. He left by himself around nine to go buy some beer. He was gone about twenty minutes. And it's only five minutes from Andy Milcher's house, where they were playing, to the nearest 7-Eleven."

"Don't sound good," I said.

"No, it don't. Milton."

"Yeah, Emmett?"

"I've known Luther Babcock all his life. Me and his big brother played together on the Cougars. And you know what, Milt?"

"What's that, Emmett?"

"He always was a snot-nosed little s.o.b."

"Well, Emmett, looks like he's graduated to the big time."

"Don't it though?"

"You need me for anything?"

"Moral support, maybe. I'm going over to his house at three this afternoon to confront him. You wanna come along?"

No. I didn't want to come along. I didn't want to be present when the police chief accused a leading citizen of murdering his mother-in-law and doing unspeakable things to the poor lady's body. I didn't want to see the look on the wife's face, the disbelief shadowed with doubt, and I didn't want to see the fear in the faces of the children. Especially the boy's who'd have to be thinking, if my Daddy could do this, what will I be capable of?

No, I didn't want a goddamn thing to do with any of it. I had enough on my hands with the two real rape/strangulations in my county, without having to deal with this sick copycat. But Emmett Hopkins and I had been friends ever since I joined the Sheriff's Department, back when it had been housed at the courthouse. We used to go to lunch together a lot back then, when he'd been just a cop on the city force. I'm the only one who knew that he'd messed around with Lydia Moore, the police department's dispatcher, during her divorce. I'm the one he told his guilt to, and agonized over his wife's finding out. I'm the one he got drunk with when he found out his only son had leukemia. And he's the one that listened to me bitch about anything and everything going on in my life.

In his three years as chief of police of Longbranch, this was his first murder case. And by now I was an old hand at it, with four under my belt, if you counted Barnie Littlefield.

So, of course, I said, "Sure, Emmett. Why'd don't I meet you at your station about two forty-five?"

"Thanks, Milt. I mean it. I owe you."

"You don't owe me a goddamn thing."

We hung up.

THIRTEEN

"NOW, LUTHER, you wanna tell me why it took so long to go get them beers?" Emmett asked.

We were sitting in the living room, or parlor, or whatever, of Mrs. Limone's house. No matter how long she was dead, I figured it would still be called Mrs. Limone's house. The sofa I was sitting on was as uncomfortable as you'd expect by looking at it. It was one of those Victorian jobbies, camel-backed, with lots of carved wood sticking into you in all sorts of nasty places. The coffee table looked like a good wind would topple it over, it was so fragile-looking. There was a silver set in front of us with coffee in it that Mrs. Babcock had brought out. If she'd been dressed in anything other than jeans, sweatshirt, and cowboy boots, it would have looked like a set for an Agatha Christie whodunit. I half-expected Emmett to stand up and say in a phony French accent, "And the murderer is..." But he didn't. But of course, Dame Agatha would never have written about the things Emmett was about to accuse Luther Babcock of doing.

"What do you mean?" Luther asked, all innocent-like. "I went to the store, got the beer, and went back to Andy's. Nothing mysterious about that."

"What store'd you go to?"

"The Safeway on Mercher Drive."

"Why'd you go all the way to the Safeway when you coulda gotten the beer at the 7-Eleven right down the street?"

"I don't know. I guess I wasn't thinking. We'd already gone through one six-pack." Luther laughed. "I guess I was a little tipsy."

"There was five guys at that game, Luther," Emmett said. "You can get *tipsy* on one beer?"

"Well, maybe it was two or three six-packs." And here he laughed again. "I guess I didn't want to admit to the police chief that I could have been driving under the influence."

"And being *tipsy* you figured it was safer to drive five miles out of your way to get the beer rather than just stop at the corner?"

"Ah, hell, Emmett, I don't know what I was thinking. Like I said, I was drunk. I'll admit it. I was drunk as a skunk."

"Drunk enough to come over here to the house and kill your mother-in-law?"

And that's when the room got real quiet. Then Luther Babcock let out a hoot and said, "What?" real loud. "What the hell are you talking about, Emmett?"

"What I'm saying to you, Luther, is that your mother-in-law didn't die by the hand of the rapist that's been going around here lately. What I'm saying is, that what with Mrs. Babcock here inheriting everything of her mother's, more'n likely, you look like a real good candidate for a copycat killer. Course, this is just my opinion, mind."

I couldn't help sneaking a peek at Amanda Babcock. She was just standing there, the blood drained from her face, looking as gray as her little old mother had yesterday. And it dawned on me that she knew. She didn't want to know, but she knew.

While I was looking at his wife, Luther Babcock had stood up. He was rigid and his face was a high color, whether from anger, fear, or too much good food, I wasn't sure. He pointed dramatically at the door. "Get out of here, Emmett. Take your sorry story and get out of my house."

"Your house, Luther?" Emmett said, standing and heading for the door, with me on his heels. "I thought this was your mother-in-law's house?"

With that we left.

In the car, I told Emmett, "His wife believes it. You see her face?"

"No, that's what I had you there for."

"Well, she went gray, I'm telling you. She believed it. Think she may have even thought about it before we got there."

Emmett nodded his head as he swerved to miss a chughole in the street. "How'm I gonna prove it, though?"

"Check with the neighbors, see if anybody saw him coming back earlier than he says last night." I'm a great one for checking our neighbors, I am.

"Yeah. And if nobody did? 'Cause if I was gonna do something like that, Milt, I'd sure as hell make sure nobody saw me. And Luther Babcock may be a lot of things, but he's never been real stupid."

"Well, would he have had time to go all the way to the Safeway and still kill his mother-in-law?" I asked.

"Hmm," Emmett thought for a minute then said, "Probably not."

"And did he actually show up with some beer?"

"Yeah, the boys at the poker party said he did."

"Okay. So where'd he get the beer?"

"At the 7-Eleven after all?"

"Maybe. Unless he had a six-pack at home."

"Well, that'd screw it. The Safeway gets too much business to remember if Luther Babcock came in to buy beer. Just 'cause nobody recognized him wouldn't mean diddly."

"That's true."

We rode in silence the rest of way to the courthouse. Pulling into his assigned parking spot right next to the back entrance to the building, Emmett said, "Milton, I know he done it. But what if I can't prove it?"

"Don't think about that, Emmett. Just keep plodding away. That's all any of us can do. You'll find something." I said this with an easy voice and a pat on his shoulder. But we both knew I was lying. Hell, I had two unsolved murders on my hands and not a clue in sight. Who'd I think I was kidding?

I left him and got back into my squad car to head for the new building. It was after four. I needed to check in before I went home and got drunk.

Everybody was there when I got in. Mike didn't have anything new from his discussion with Bill Williams in Tejas County. Dalton just kept shaking his head and trying not to think about the two little girls whose bodies he'd had to help pick up off the highway the day before, and Berle was still depressed about all the little old ladies he'd seen yesterday morning and how scared they'd all been. We all sat in the big deputy bullpen and told each other how miserable we were.

And then Gladys said, "When's Chicken Little gonna come running in here yelling, 'The sky is falling, the sky is falling'?" And laughed.

We all looked at her. For Gladys, that was a hell of a joke. The first any of us had ever heard from her. We sat in stunned silence and watched as she loaded up her purse and walked out the door, still chuckling to herself.

"Well, I'll be goddamned," Berle said, and we all nodded our heads in agreement.

Mrs. Horne was raking leaves when I pulled into the driveway. I got out and took the rake out of her hands.

"Let me do this, Miz Horne," I said. "I need the exercise."

She smiled. "Thank you, Mr. Kovak. How 'bout some iced tea?"

I thanked her and she went inside her house to fix us both a glass. I raked the leaves that had fallen from her pecan trees, and picked up scattered pecans and put them in my pocket as a reward. Half an hour and two glasses of iced tea later, I had me three nice piles of leaves and my pockets sagging with nuts. Feeling a little guilty, I showed Mrs. Horne what I had in my pockets. She laughed.

"Lordy, Mr. Kovak, that's not enough pecans to do anything with 'cept eat. And I never did like eating pecans raw. Always tasted dusty to me. You're welcome to 'em."

I thanked her and went into my half of the house and got out a light beer and my nutcracker. I wished she hadn't said that about the nuts tasting dusty because I'd never noticed it before. But they did. It took a whole six-pack to wash them down. And drinking that six-pack made me wonder about that six-pack Luther Babcock had taken back to the poker party. And I had me a germ of an idea.

While I was considering the possibilities, the phone rang.

"Mr. Kovak? This is Miz Horne."

"Yes, ma'am?"

"Could you come over here right away?"

I'm not sure but I think I may have left the phone off the hook in my dash for her part of the house. I drew my gun and charged in her front door in my socks. And stood there like an idiot and watched the smiles fade and the eyes get big on the faces of Mrs. Horne; her cousin, the sheriff's mother; and Mrs. Nadine Blankenship, who were all three holding on to a great big birthday cake with forty-eight candles blazing away. It was my birthday. I'd forgotten. The wife hadn't been around to remind me.

Mrs. Nadine Blankenship spoke first. "Deputy, you wanna put that thing away?"

"Yes, ma'am," I said, holstering my gun. There are times in your life when you feel like a complete fool because you are a complete fool. This was one of those times.

"Well," said the other Mrs. Blankenship, the sheriff's mother. "Happy Birthday."

"Thank you," I managed to get out. I figured of all people, the sheriff must have remembered my birthday and sent his women around to do something about it. None of the deputies had remembered, not even Gladys, who was real big on birthdays and such.

Laura didn't even know. But the sheriff had remembered, and that made me feel kind of nice.

"Take that rig off and go put it on the mantel, where you can reach it if Iranian terrorists decide to invade," Mrs. Nadine Blankenship said. "A party's no place for it."

I obeyed and took off the holster and gun and placed them carefully on the mantel. And then we got down to the party. Mrs. Horne had made a three-layer chocolate cake decorated with tiny blue roses with my name written in frosting in the center. I was touched. We cut the cake so that everybody got a rose. Then they brought out the presents. Mrs. Horne gave me a Bible with my name embossed in gold at the bottom, and Mrs. Blankenship the elder gave me a Cross pen-and-pencil set. Nadine Blankenship gave me a gold tie-clip shaped like a tiny pair of handcuffs. I'd seen it in a journal once. You can buy a lot of stuff like that.

"It was Elberry's idea," she explained. I thanked them all and did my best not to burst into tears.

The next morning, I called Emmett and told him my notion. He agreed to meet me at Mrs. Limone's house.

Luther had gone back to work. He ran the furniture store that had been owned by the Limone family for three generations. He had some things to take care of before the funeral, which was to be held Saturday morning. The kids had gone back to school, and Amanda Limone Babcock was all alone in her house with her thoughts. I figured this would be a good time to find out what her thoughts were.

She opened the door for us and we shook hands. Amanda Limone had been about as pretty as her mother, which wasn't saying much. She resembled a horse in a lot of ways, and not one of the ways being a horse's grace and beauty. She was tall and skinny and all you really noticed about her body was knees and elbows. Her face was long and her hair was cut short in a way that only accentuated the length of that horsey face. Luther Babcock, tall, good-looking, blond and blue-eyed, must have been quite a catch for this tall, gawky woman.

The way I figured it, Luther Babcock had married for money. He married a not very pretty lady with a widowed mother who was an invalid. And who had remained an invalid for the fifteen years of their marriage. The way I figured it, Luther Babcock just got tired of waiting for the old lady to die a natural death. And he took advantage of the fact that I had a rapist around that I couldn't catch. That made it personal with me.

Mrs. Babcock showed us into the parlor. I avoided the sofa I'd sat on yesterday and chose instead a wingback chair covered in real leather, soft as an old saddle. I figured having a chair like this in my half of Mrs. Horne's house would definitely improve my posture. The back was so straight I was almost leaning forward. I wondered where these people went to get comfortable.

"What can I do for you, Chief Deputy?" Mrs. Babcock asked. She was sitting on the edge of the sofa, knees close together, wearing what looked like the same jeans and sweatshirt of the day before. Her feet, though, were bare, and I noticed that her toes were long, with great big bulbs on the ends. Seriously ugly feet. I started to correct her and say, "Acting

Sheriff,'' but as this wasn't my jurisdiction, I figured, what the hell?

"Mrs. Babcock," Emmett said, "I hate to intrude on you like this, but I have a few questions I need answers to. I was hoping you'd help me out."

"Certainly. Anything I can do." Her voice was a flat monotone and she looked like somebody in shock. I didn't envy Emmett his job at that minute.

"I was wondering, Mrs. Babcock, if, when you go grocery shopping, if you buy beer as a rule?"

"Yes."

"And when was the last time you went grocery shopping, Mrs. Babcock?"

"I went to the store Wednesday to pick up a few things."

"Did you buy any beer?"

"Yes. We were all out of beer. Luther likes his beer in the evening."

"How many six-packs did you buy, Mrs. Babcock?"

"Three."

"And how many were left yesterday, ma'am?"

She heaved a great big sigh. She'd been waiting for this, it was obvious. Now all we needed to know was whether or not she'd tell the truth. But how many women would when it meant their husband's very lives? Maybe one out of ten, I figured, and luckily, Amanda Limone Babcock was that one.

"There was one six-pack and part of another."

"Where do you think that third six-pack went, ma'am?"

She'd been looking at her ugly toes during this whole time. With that question, she looked up at Emmett and then looked over at me. Finally, she turned back to Emmett and said, "I don't know, Chief."

"Mrs. Babcock—" Emmett started, but she stood up and walked toward the door.

"If that's all, Chief Hopkins, I have arrangements to make for my mother's funeral."

We'd been dismissed and we knew it. But we had what Emmett needed. I drove with him in his chief-of-police car to the Limone Furniture Store on Crosby Road. I noticed on the way that his engine was missing and figured the city was going through the same cutbacks as the county. I felt a little better about that.

We pulled into the public parking lot of the store and walked in the front door and through the cheap furniture that I'm sure never saw its way into Mrs. Limone's house. The furniture the Limones sold was for the masses, not for the likes of the Limones.

Luther Babcock's office was in the back of the store. A clerk tried to bar our way, but Emmett showed his badge and the clerk moved aside. We went in without knocking and Emmett arrested Luther Babcock for the murder of his mother-in-law, taking the little slip of paper out of his pocket that had the writing on it to read him his rights.

At that moment I envied the hell out of my old friend Emmett Hopkins. What I wouldn't have done to be reading somebody his rights I wouldn't want to say. Emmett had his killer, with my help. But I still didn't have mine. I wondered what the sheriff was going to say when he found out I'd helped the city police find their killer. It didn't bear imagining.

But I found out as soon as I got back to the station. How the sheriff got the news in the short time it took me to get from the courthouse to the new building I'll never know, because he didn't go about enlightening me on that. He just said, "Well, now, boy, you done real good. When you going to work for the Long-branch Police on a paying basis?"

"Hey, Sheriff," I said, "how you doing?"

"Oh, I'm just fine, boy. Being shot's a hell of a lot of fun. You oughta try it."

Which was a downright nasty thing for the sheriff to say and I was getting tired of making allowances for the fact that he was sick and I was to blame for his being sick. There's only so much guilt a body can handle before it starts rejecting it.

So I said, "Yeah, maybe I will. When I go to work for Emmett Hopkins. At twenty-five hundred dollars more a year then you're paying me."

"Says who?"

"Says Emmett." Now, of course, Emmett had never said any such thing, but I was pissed the sheriff was pissed and that's the way these things go.

He laughed. "Boy, if you can get that tight-assed city council to pay you half of what I'm paying you, you'll be doing great. Meanwhile"—and here he stopped laughing—"why don't you buckle down and find me that rapist and let Emmett Hopkins worry about his own little problems. Hear me, boy?"

"Oh, I hear you, Elberry. But I also heard that speech you made at the last Rotary meeting, all about the spirit of cooperation between us and the city po-lice. Or were you just passing wind?"

"I don't know if the acting sheriff title's gone to your head or if you're just stupider than I ever gave you credit for, Milton, but you're treading on real thin ice.''

And I knew it. Now in the city they got this thing called midlife crisis, or male menopause, or some such. I'd read about it in one of the wife's *Reader's Digest* magazines. I think it had something to do with aging yuppies, but I'm not sure. But I was beginning to think maybe I'd caught it. From all those trips to Tulsa maybe.

I took a couple of deep breaths, sighed, and said, ''Sheriff, you're right. I'm sorry. But as for helping Emmett, I gotta tell you I'd do it again. I wish to God I could get a lead on our little sicko, Sheriff, but I'm dead out of leads. And all me and the coroner had to do was walk in that death room and we knew it wasn't our guy. Was I not supposed to tell Emmett that?''

I heard a sigh on the other end of the line. ''Course not, Milt. Guess I'm just pissed 'cause his department's looking better than mine.''

''Not our fault this guy ain't hitting anybody for real in Longbranch.''

''True. But the voters aren't gonna see it that way.''

''Sheriff—''

''Milt, I'm tired. I gotta go rest.''

And he hung up. And I sat in his office pretending I was in charge and feeling like homemade shit.

That evening I went home and changed into some grubbies and fixed some tuna fish and grabbed a light beer. Then I sat down on the sofa with my feet propped up on the coffee table and ate half my sandwich while Evinrude ate the other half, and drank my beer and watched the TV. I was on the last beer of my six-pack when the "Late Show" came on. It was an old movie called *Obsession* and I watched it and thought about Laura Johnson and told Evinrude that old Cliff Robertson didn't have a thing on me.

FOURTEEN

NOW FATE'S a funny little puppy, you know? If Miss Sue Ellen Gilmore hadn't finally decided to forgive her brother Ervin for falling asleep during the church service at the Holy Trinity Bible Church the last time he visited her in Bishop two years ago, then he wouldn't have been down here again from Ardmore to visit on the anniversary of their mama's death forty years before. And if Ervin Gilmore hadn't been down here visiting from Ardmore, then his sister Sue Ellen would be dead.

Now Miss Sue Ellen generally lives alone. Except when her brother Ervin is visiting. And Miss Sue Ellen hadn't told anybody that Ervin was coming to visit because she was still a little mad at him and didn't want any of her friends to know that she had weakened after only two years.

On Monday night, October 24, at about nine-thirty, while I was rolling around on the floor of the windowed room with my lady love, Ervin Gilmore was resting his eyes in front of the TV in the back room of his sister's home, the home that used to be his mama's. He had an earjack on because the noise of the TV, which he had to turn up loud on account of his loss of hearing, bothered his sister, who was in the front bedroom trying to sleep.

Halfway through "Cagney and Lacey," he heard a noise but figured it was a car or dog outside, so ig-

nored it. Then he heard it again. Now Ervin Gilmore
doesn't like to move any more than necessary. He
broke a hip three years ago last May and walks with a
cane, and getting up out of a chair is not a whole lot
of fun. But the noise began to bother him, so he went
to investigate.

And that's when he found his little sister on the bed
in the front bedroom with a man straddling her, his
hands around her throat. And Miss Sue Ellen Gilmore was turning an ugly shade of blue. So Ervin
yelled and held on to one of the four-posters of the bed
that had come over from Germany with Great-
granddaddy Hermann and used his cane to pummel
the man. He hit him in the face at one point, the back
of the head, and the arm, when the man brought it up
to shield himself. The man got off the bed, knocked
the old man down, and ran for the front door. He had
to run through the lighted living room to do that and
Ervin Gilmore got a good look at him from his position on the floor. Ervin pulled himself up and hob-
bled to the phone in the living room and called the
Sheriff's Department. I, of course, didn't know anything about it until I got back into beeper range at ten
thirty-five.

I got to the Gilmore house at ten forty-five, where
Ervin still waited. Miss Sue Ellen had been taken to the
hospital suffering from shock. He'd raped her, but she
was alive. And I just thanked God for that.

"Mr. Gilmore?" I looked down at the old man sitting on the sofa in the living room. He'd taught third
grade at the elementary school when I was a boy, and
though I'd had Mrs. Sumner instead of him, I remembered him. He'd seemed older than God then,

and now I knew he had to be well into his nineties. Which would make his little sister somewhere in her late eighties. When he retired from schoolteaching, he'd moved to Ardmore for some reason to do with his wife's family. He had been tall and thin when I was a boy, now he was short and thin. That's how these things go, I suppose.

He looked up at me and said, "Yes, sir?"

What goes around comes around, huh? Mr. Gilmore calling me sir. Didn't seem right. It made me sad. It made me think of how, the older you get, the more the parent becomes the child, and vice versa, if you know what I mean. It made me remember the time when Mama was in the hospital and she wet herself and she begged me to change her so the nurses wouldn't see what she'd done. I'd gone home and cried like a baby after that. Somehow, I felt like crying now. Mr. Gilmore calling me sir.

I sat down next to him on the sofa and patted his scrawny shoulder. "You okay, Mr. Gilmore?" His color was high and I was worried about that.

"I'm okay," he said in a voice that sounded like a thin shadow of the voice I could remember coming through the thin wall of the school, shouting at the third graders in his class to straighten up or get the ruler.

"You saw this guy, Mr. Gilmore?"

"Yes, sir, I saw him."

"Can you describe him for me?"

The old man took a deep breath and squinted at me where I sat next to him. "Well, he was a young fella. Younger than you. Taller than me. Stocky. Dark hair, all wiry-like, and curly." He shook his head. "That's all I remember."

"After he ran out, did you hear a car start up?"

He shook his head and pointed at his left ear. "My hearing's not what it used to be. Sorry."

"What was he wearing?"

He looked toward the ceiling for a minute, then shook his head. "I don't know. Ah . . . a shirt? Yeah. Blue, I think. Light blue. And pants. Blue jeans, I think."

"A jacket?"

He shook his head again. "Don't remember seeing one."

"What about shoes?"

He shrugged his bony shoulders. "I didn't look at his feet, Sheriff."

I didn't correct him. It hardly seemed worth the effort.

"When he ran out, did you hear the clump of heavy boots, something like that?"

Again he shrugged. "Not that I remember." He stopped for a moment, then smiled at me. "He was wearing high-topped black sneakers. Like kids used to do. Remember those high-topped sneakers?"

I nodded my head.

"That's what he was wearing. I remember now. From where I was on the floor, that's what I saw first before I looked up at the rest of him. High-topped black sneakers. Like kids used to wear."

I returned his smile and patted his shoulder. "Anything else, Mr. Gilmore?"

He shook his head, then grinned at me. "Think maybe he'll have a black eye tomorrow, though. I got him a good lick with my cane in the face. On his left side."

"That's the best news I've heard all year, Mr. Gilmore. I'm glad you got him."

Ervin Gilmore's face became grim. "Just wish I coulda killed the son of a bitch."

I didn't say I wished he had too.

I thanked him and asked Mike, who was the first on the scene, to take him to County Memorial and have the doctors check him for shock. I sure didn't like that high color he had.

I poked around Miss Sue Ellen's house for a while, not finding much of anything but thinking mostly about the man in the green Chevy. Who had been blond. I figured we'd been looking for the wrong guy. But things were looking up.

As late as it was, I still decided to drop by the sheriff's house. And it was a good thing I did.

When Mrs. Blankenship opened the door, she said, "Thank God you came by. He's been beating the ear of that poor A.B. at the station ever since he heard. He's on the phone now, back in the bedroom."

I went down the hall and opened the door to the master bedroom. When the sheriff saw me, he said into the phone, "Never mind, A.B., Milt's here now. But you call me the minute you hear anything new."

He hung up and turned toward me. He was flushed with excitement and the fringe of hair around his head was standing out every which way.

"'Bout goddamn time you got here! So tell me everything!"

And I did.

"So your witness was full of shit all along," he said when I'd finished, which I resented but I figured I'd better not show it unless I felt like explaining it, which I didn't, if you know what I mean.

"Yeah, well, I guess the guy Mrs. Johnson saw was up there for some other reason. Unless we got us two rapists, which I'd just as soon not even consider."

The sheriff nodded. "Not worth considering. So where do you go now?"

"I've got all the deputies except A.B. out combing the neighborhood. But we're getting closer, Sheriff. No doubt about that."

"'Close' only counts in horseshoes and hand grenades, boy. I want that asshole in the lockup, where we can get nostalgic with him."

"Nostalgic?"

"Yeah, show him what it was like in the good old days, when we could beat the shit out of a suspect."

He grinned and I tried to grin back, knowing—hoping—he was only kidding.

After another few minutes, Mrs. Blankenship came in and threw me out, so I went on home to my half of Mrs. Horne's house. And spent the rest of the night avoiding thoughts of the dark, curly-haired rapist by thinking of Laura and the night we'd had together.

It had been the best night ever. I had gotten there early enough that the kids were still up, and we'd all had supper together. They were full of school talk and plans for costumes come Halloween. They wanted me to dress up and take them trick-or-treating. Which I didn't know how to answer since I didn't know where Laura's husband would be. But she answered for me.

"Maybe we can drive into town and stop by and see Uncle Milt," she said. Which I knew meant that wherever her husband would be that night, he wouldn't be trick-or-treating with his children.

"Great!" was Trent's reply and Rebecca said, "Will you make us a neat treat, Uncle Milt? Like caramel apples or popcorn balls? And will you dress up real scary like a skeleton or something and scare us? And will you have your house all dark, with witches and things, and do you have a cat?"

I agreed to everything including the cat and wondered how Evinrude would take to dress-up. I figured he probably wouldn't take to it at all. I figured he'd probably decide it was high time for another four-day outing.

Trent and Rebecca cleaned up the kitchen, which was something they were just learning how to do, and after we got them in bed, Laura and I went back downstairs and cleaned up the mess of their cleaning up. Then we sat by the fire and talked and talked until she touched me or I touched her, whichever, and we ended up in the windowed room on the floor under her afghan.

Being with Laura. How can words describe being with Laura? I'm not a poet or maybe I could do it. I wish I was. I wish I could write a sonnet about how her body feels under my hand, about the smoothness of her skin and hardness of her nipples when I touch them with my lips. I wish I could write an ode to her moans, her squeals of delight. But I can't do any of those things. I'm not a poet. I'm just a portly, balding deputy sheriff in love. Sounds like a country-and-western song title, don't it?

Tuesday I let some of the deputies go home and sleep till noon while the rest were out combing the area for the dark curly-haired rapist with a black eye. At noon, I sent the first shift home and the second shift took over. But it didn't do any good. We didn't find anything. We didn't find clues, or tire tracks, or a dark curly-haired rapist with a black eye. We didn't find diddly-squat, which was something I was almost getting used to.

After two days, it was business as usual, with a car wreck on the interstate and another case of canned peaches stolen, this time from Tatem's Kwik Stop on Highway 5. I was getting to the point where I was fantasizing about finding a dark curly-haired man with a black eye eating a can of peaches.

I went to choir practice on Wednesday night and walked Mrs. Richards home and avoided talking about God calling anybody home for whatever reason. We talked about Halloween instead, and how much better it had been when we were both young.

In her day, the big thing had been knocking over outhouses. In my day, it had been soaping windows. But in both days, kids were allowed to run free on Halloween night and not worry about getting treats laced with heroin, apples with long needles shoved down inside them, or pennies that had been roasted over an open fire. Nowadays, the churches and schools had carnivals on Halloween so that parents could bring their kids there instead of taking the chance of them meeting a neighbor who wasn't quite sane.

I looked forward to the kids coming to my house on Halloween, and on Thursday, during my lunch hour,

I went over to the K Mart on the interstate and bought decorations and caramel and a silly, scary mask to wear. It was the first time I would celebrate the scary holiday since I was fourteen years old, when I stopped because it wasn't the cool thing to do anymore. Now, celebrating Halloween with Laura and her children seemed to be the coolest thing in the world to do. I was invested heavy with Laura Johnson, but that didn't bear thinking about.

On Friday, the whole world tilted, did a little jig then turned upside down. I was walking with Dalton to the Longbranch Inn for lunch when Laura, with Adam on one hip, stepped out of the door of the five-and-dime with a bag under her free arm. And next to her, holding two TG & Y bags, was a dark curly-haired man with yellowing skin around his left eye, the kind of yellowing skin you get when a four-day-old bruise is healing.

I stopped and stared like an idiot. She stopped too, but recovered fast.

"Deputy Kovak! Nice to see you! I don't think you've ever met my husband. Jerry, this is the deputy that was working on Mrs. Munsky's murder."

Jerry Johnson shook my hand and smiled. It took a lot of effort, but I managed to do the same.

FIFTEEN

DALTON AND I walked on to the Longbranch Inn and found a table. It was crowded for a weekday, then I remembered there'd been a County Home Ec meeting in town that day, with all the high school 4-H'ers in the county showing up with their sponsors. And they'd all decided to take lunch at the Longbranch Inn.

We sat down, with Dalton talking a mile a minute about something, but I wasn't paying any attention. All I could think about was Laura. And her husband. And inside I was so scared I couldn't think straight. Laura's husband was the rapist. My beautiful Laura was living with a killer and didn't even know it.

But it all fit. Monday nights. Every Monday night while I was humping his wife, Jerry Johnson was out killing old ladies. Why? Why would anybody who had somebody like Laura do this? Then I remembered what I'd read on a flyer one time sent out by the Rape Crisis Coalition of Tulsa. Rape wasn't an act of sex, it was an act of violence.

And I now knew who was perpetrating that violence. Only me. Nobody else knew, except Jerry Johnson. And what was I going to do with that information?

I had to go slow. Think it through. I had to prove it beyond a shadow of a doubt. The old man, Ervin Gilmore, might be able to identify Jerry Johnson.

Then again he might not. He'd been through a lot, and he was very, very old.

Miss Sue Ellen might be able to identify him, except she had slipped into a coma before ever coming out of shock, and the doctors at County Memorial doubted she would ever come out of it. And even if she did, it had been dark in that bedroom.

I had to prove it, without anybody knowing what I was doing. Because I wanted all the *i*'s dotted and all the *t*'s crossed on this one. Jerry Johnson wasn't going to slip through on some technicality. I had to get him so good that there was no way he'd ever bother Laura and the kids again. I wanted to hand the sheriff this one on a platter, all tied up with a pretty pink ribbon, if you'll excuse the mixed metaphor.

I had to get ahold of the Swensen's Farm Machinery travel vouchers and find out where Jerry Johnson had been on each of the nights of the murders. Without anybody knowing why I was doing it. And I had to do all this before Halloween night. Because Halloween was on a Monday.

And then I remembered. When Mrs. Munsky had been killed I'd called Swensen's Farm Machinery to find out about Jerry Johnson's whereabouts on a whim of the sheriff's. And he had been out of town. Had he not killed Mrs. Munsky? Were there two murderers? I was getting confused and wished I could talk to the sheriff about this one. But I couldn't. Not yet.

"You gonna eat them sweet potatoes?"

"What?" I looked up at Dalton's question. He was eyeing me in that semithere fashion of his. "You want my sweet potatoes?"

"Only if you ain't gonna eat 'em, Milt."

"Go head. Eat my sweet potatoes."

I shoved the plate at him in a half-pissed, half-abstracted way and got up from the table and left the Longbranch Inn, almost not noticing that Glenda Sue Robertson was saying hi.

I walked back to the Sheriff's Department, not seeing the beautiful day or the people in the streets. Somebody said hi to me and I nodded back but didn't notice who it was. My Laura and my kids were living with a killer. That's all that kept going through my mind.

I had to get Jerry Johnson out of that house. The fact that he'd never hurt them yet, that he took all his craziness out on little old ladies didn't stop me from worrying about their safety. And it didn't stop me from worrying about the effect this was going to have on Trent and Rebecca and Adam when they realized what their daddy did when he wasn't home.

I had to have a reason for looking at the travel vouchers at Swensen's Farm Machinery. And I didn't have one. Swensen's was a block outside the city limits of Longbranch, which made it county jurisdiction. But it was a clean little operation and there was no reason to go there at all.

I was home in my half of Mrs. Horne's house and on my third beer when it came to me. A reason for looking through the records of Swensen's Farm Machinery. If they were to have a burglary, then there'd be a reason for the Sheriff's Department to investigate. And investigating a burglary could mean looking through all sorts of records, if you wanted to stretch a point. But I didn't have time to wait for na-

ture to take its course and Swensen's to be burglar-
ized. I was just going to have to do it myself.

Now, I've always been a law-abiding citizen. Hell,
I'm a deputy sheriff, sworn to uphold the law. The one
time I'd hired an accountant to do my taxes and he'd
stretched a point here and there, I'd gone home and
redone it so it would be right. When the wife's car
broke on her way to visit her mother in Bishop, I drove
her over in the squad car and felt so guilty about it I
put five dollars in the petty-cash fund to cover the gas.
Don't tell me about Jewish guilt and Catholic guilt,
'cause I can tell you a heap about Baptist guilt.

So here I was, the most law-abiding citizen *I've* ever
known, planning to break into Swensen's Farm Machinery and fudge a burglary. Don't that beat all?

So I put on the pants of my dark wool suit and a
navy-blue pullover shirt and a dark-brown cardigan
the wife'd bought me a few years ago that I never
wear. And I pulled a navy-blue watch cap over my
light-brown hair. I didn't smear my face with shoe
polish, but I suppose you get the picture. I borrowed
an ax out of Mrs. Horne's garage and went out to the
'55 and got in and started the car, feeling a little tipsy,
as Luther Babcock might say, and a whole lot scared.

I drove the two and a half miles to Swensen's Farm
Machinery and went on past it, pulling up in front of
the Bingo Parlor where there were a lot of cars and
mine wouldn't stand out. But I had to finish before
ten-thirty, when all those nice anonymous cars were
going to leave. I got out of the car, pulling on gloves,
then taking the ax and holding it with the handle up
the sleeve of my cardigan and the head resting in my
hand. I walked as nonchalantly as possible in the other

direction from Swensen's, past the Rexall Pharmacy on the corner of Crosby and College, the other side of which is where the city limits starts. I turned on College and went down the street, looking around before I dipped into the alley that ran behind the store and the Bingo Parlor. The alley emptied out into the parking lot of Swensen's, where there were absolutely no cars. Which was good news and bad news. Good news because that meant nobody was there, bad news because I didn't have anything to hide behind. If I was going to cross the hundred feet to Swensen's building, I was going to do it in plain sight.

My palms were sweating so badly the ax head almost slipped. My pulse was racing and I could feel my heart thumping through my shirt. I figured this wasn't a smart thing for an overweight, forty-eight-year-old man to be doing. I just hoped I wouldn't drop dead of a heart attack in the empty parking lot of Swensen's Farm Machinery with an ax up my sleeve. It could be embarrassing for the sheriff. And being the ex-wife of a possible ax murderer wouldn't do the wife's position in the community a bit of good.

The night air was crisp and there was a full moon. I could have done without that. I kept walking through the parking lot to the near side of the building, where I slipped into the shadows and turned to look at where I'd just been. I could see part of the front of the Bingo Parlor, and all the cars, including my '55, still sat there nice as you please. Nobody was standing in the street pointing at me. Which I took to be a good sign.

I crept around to the back of the building to the back door, where I could see the machinery for the night alarm. I took the ax out of my sleeve and whacked mightily at the door handle with the head. The metal-on-metal sound vibrated through the still night air. It sounded about as loud as a fart in church. The alarm didn't go off. So I hit it again. And then again. And then the door popped open and still the goddamn alarm didn't go off.

Being a deputy sheriff, you know about things like alarms. And this one I knew wasn't a silent alarm. This was one of those loud alarms that wake up the neighborhood and also sound off at the Sheriff's Department. And this one was just sitting there not doing a goddamn thing.

So I pushed the back door of Swensen's Farm Machinery with my foot and walked warily in. The back door opened into a warehouse full of tractors and crates of what I supposed was farm machinery. I didn't feel up to lifting the crates or the tractors, so I went on forward until I got to the office. The office was full of small stuff like computers and electric typewriters and an expensive-looking radio. I left the radio in case it was a personal item of one of the employees and took a typewriter under one arm and part of a computer under the other. And that's when the goddamn alarm went off.

Now, knowing that it would take A.B. a good fifteen minutes to get around to responding to the alarm didn't do my heart a whole hell of a lot of good. That typewriter was heavy as shit, I want you to know. But I managed to run the length of that warehouse like Jesse Owens in his prime and got me the hell out of there. I threw the typewriter and the part of the computer into the Dipsy Dumpster in the back parking lot and made it to the shadows of the alley behind the Bingo Parlor without dying.

Now all I had to do was get home and wait for the call and tomorrow I'd inspect the travel vouchers that would start to set up the case against Jerry Johnson.

SIXTEEN

WHEN I PULLED INTO the driveway of Mrs. Horne's house, there was a city police car sitting there and I almost peed in my pants. I swear to God. Then I saw Emmett walking toward me from my little porch and grinning.

"Hey, Emmett," I said, slipping out of the car after stashing the watch cap, the gloves, and the ax under the seat.

"Hey, Milt, where you been?"

I hoped to hell it was one of those rhetorical questions you read about.

I grinned back at him as best I could and said, "Oh, just out and about. What're you up to?"

"Friday-night tomcatting, huh? Jeez, you bachelors. Must be nice! Thought you might have a beer you wanted to get rid of."

I took my keys out of my pocket and opened the door to my half of Mrs. Horne's house. "All I have is one of them light beers, tastes like piss and water, but you're welcome to it."

"Light beer? Hell, Milt, and all this time I thought you was a real man." And he laughed like a hyena and I wondered what time it was and whether that laugh would wake up Mrs. Horne.

So I popped a top for both of us and we settled down on my new used sofa and I wondered but didn't ask what the hell he was doing there, tonight of all nights.

Finally, he said, "Milt, I just wanted to thank you in private for your help on that Luther Babcock thing."

I did my Gary Cooper imitation and said, "Ah, hell, Emmett, wasn't much of anything." There was no dust for me to scrape my toe in but I guess you get the general idea.

"No, I mean it, Milt; if it hadn't been for you, I'da been busting my ass from now till the cows come home and getting exactly zip."

"Well, Emmett," I lied, "you know the sheriff has a policy of complete cooperation with the city force. We were just pleased as punch that we could help out a little bit."

And to this Emmett let out a snort. "Oh, yeah, El-berry's real big on cooperation. Bet he chewed your ass out good on this one."

Well, there are two kinds of loyalty, one to your employer and one to your friend. And since Emmett was my friend, but the sheriff was both my employer and my friend, I figured he won out on this one.

"The sheriff was real pleased I could help you out, Emmett."

Emmett snorted again but didn't press the point. He slugged down the rest of his beer and stood up. And held out his hand. "Well, whatever, Milt. But any-way, thanks." We shook and he left, with me having to go out to the driveway and move the '55 so he could get his squad car out of the drive. Then I went back into my apartment and proceeded to start sweating. I figured I'd put it off too long.

I'd had my beeper in my pocket the whole time I'd been out and about and it hadn't gone off. And after thirty minutes back at the house, the phone still hadn't rung. And I couldn't wait anymore so I called the station.

"Prophesy County Sheriff's Department," A.B. said as he picked up the phone.

"Hey, A.B., it's Milt. How's it going?"

"Oh, hidy, Milt. Everything's just fine?"

Wonderful. "Okay, well, I'm hitting the bed now, but if you need me, just call. Okay, A.B?"

"Okay, Milt. Good night and don't let the bed bugs bite."

So I hung up and sat in my burglar clothes on the sofa and wondered why in the hell he hadn't mentioned that the alarm had gone off at Swensen's. Then I figured that as the alarm was broken enough not to go off when I first broke in, maybe it was broken enough not to go off at the sheriff's office. And maybe I'd have to wait until morning, unless some good citizen had heard that screeching and turned it in.

But nobody did. And it was eight-fifteen in the morning before somebody from Swensen's called. I had gotten to the station bright and early at seven-thirty, on a Saturday, which raised some eyebrows, to wait for the call, hoping like hell that somebody'd be working some overtime at Swensen's. By eight I figured maybe I'd hallucinated the whole thing.

But then the call came, and like a good acting sheriff, I was immediately on the scene.

The only problem was that there weren't just a typewriter and part of a computer missing. Two tractors, a crate of attachments, and the radio were missing too. I figured some good citizen had heard the alarm after all and managed to turn it off. And helped himself while he was about it. I felt real bad about that.

But not bad enough not to do what I'd come for. I told Wayne Swensen, the owner, that maybe it could be a disgruntled employee and maybe I should look through his records. Wayne was tickled pink to show me where they were. And he walked out and shut the door and left me to it. Which was a nice thing for him to do.

After the door shut behind him, I left the file on terminated employees and headed for the file cabinet that said "Travel Vouchers." That's the one I wanted and I blessed the secretary that had labeled it so good. In my pocket I had the copy I had made of the sheriff's blackboard musings, so I pulled it out and checked the vouchers in as methodical a manner as my pounding heart would let me. And this is what I found out.

On April 12, Jerry Johnson had eaten dinner at the Kingsfield Café in Tabor County, a four-mile drive from Lauden, where Mrs. Coreen Middleburg had been killed. I wrote down all the other places he'd been on Tuesdays from April 12 until June 7, when the next murder had occurred. Most of the places he'd been were way out of range for our having heard about any murders. Once he'd been in a place near Oklahoma City, once down in Ardmore, once in Lawton, and once in Sherman, Texas, I figured I'd call the authorities in those places when I got back to the station and see if they had any unsolved murders for those dates.

On June 7, the Tuesday night when Miss Irene Brown had been killed, he'd been in Tejas County. Every one of the times fit, until I got to Beatrice Munsky. On that date, according to the receptionist I'd talked to at the time, he was supposed to have been in Bulger in Tabor County, but there were no travel vouchers for meals on that day. And then I did the smartest thing I'd done since I got on the case. I walked over to the file labeled "Sick Leave" and pulled it open. One of these days, I'm gonna grow up to be a real-live law-enforcement officer, I swear to God.

I found the file on Jerry Johnson and sure enough, he'd been home sick on Monday, August 15, instead of in Bulger. But then why hadn't Laura told me that? Because she didn't know. Because he wasn't at home at all that day, he was at Mrs. Munsky's.

I found the little secretary whose radio had been stolen (I thought maybe I'd go by the K Mart later that afternoon and pick one up and send it to her anonymously—talk about your Baptist guilt) and asked her where the Xerox machine was. She showed me to it and I made copies of everything I needed and headed back to the station, figuring I'd worry about the real burglary later.

I went into the sheriff's office and shut the door and looked at my notes, then called the Ardmore Police Department. Jerry Johnson had been in Ardmore on April 19. I asked the officer who answered the phone if there'd been any rape/murders in his area on or around that date. There had been none.

I tried not to worry about what the county commissioners were going to say about the long-distance telephone bill and called the agency that handled the law enforcement for Choctaw, a little town outside of Oklahoma City. Again, nothing.

Then I called the Lawton Police Department. Jerry Johnson had been in Lawton on Tuesday, May 10. On Wednesday morning, May 11, Miss Maybelle Norton had been found dead. The officer I talked to said they had had no leads and it was still an open case.

"She been raped?" I asked.

"Well, yeah."

"No semen, right?"

"How'd you know that?"

"Look, I might have something for you on this, but I gotta tie up some loose ends," I told him. "Let me get back to you."

"Where'd you say you was calling from?"

And I hung up. And then I called Sherman, Texas, where Jerry Johnson had been on May 24. And where a Mrs. Taylor had been found dead on May 25.

"But I doubt it's gonna tie into anything you got," the officer I spoke to told me. "We arrested a guy the next day and he's been down in Huntsville now for a couple of months."

"I hate to be the one to tell you this," I said, "but there's this great big possibility that there's one innocent man in Huntsville."

And I hung up. Like I said before, I'm a big believer in grand exits.

So I had opportunity. And with him being a man, I had means. And with this kind of case, motive wasn't much of a question. The guy was just crazy, and anybody could be crazy. But all I really had was opportunity. And would that hold up in court if Jerry got himself even a halfway decent attorney? I didn't want to take the chance.

So I left the Sheriff's Department and went over to County Memorial to talk to Dr. Hutchins, who wasn't there because it was Saturday. So I drove to her house, which was the kind of house you'd expect a doctor to live in. Big. Dr. Hutchins is about fifty, on the skinny side, with a look about her that said she wasn't as healthy as she ought to be. She was the only psychiatrist I knew.

After I told her what I wanted, she gave me her off-the-cuff, as she called it, psychological profile of the killer: "I'd say he has low self-esteem with possible delusions of grandeur. Probably was raised by an older woman, possibly a grandmother, great-aunt, something like that. If he wasn't physically abused as a child, he was probably neglected or emotionally or mentally abused. The lack of semen I'd say shows he's probably impotent to a degree. The attacks are a form of punishment, getting back at this old woman who had played a major role in his upbringing." She shrugged and lit a cigarette. "When you get him, Milt, I'd like a crack at him, okay?"

Leaving her house, it dawned on me I knew nothing of Laura's past. I had no idea where they had lived before moving to Mountain Falls Road. The records at Swensen's Farm Machinery showed that Jerry Johnson had joined that outfit only three years ago. And I knew they'd bought the house three years ago. It was possible, probable, that they'd moved to the area from some other town. I went back to Swensen's to look at the active employees' files.

Before coming to work for Swensen's Farm Machinery, Jerry Johnson had worked for Oilriggers, Inc., a drilling company out of Lubbock, Texas, for five years. And before that, for another company in Lubbock for three years. Looking at his résumé, I noticed that all his job history was in Lubbock. Therefore, and it didn't take a Sherlock Holmes to figure this out, Jerry Johnson was from Lubbock, Texas.

And the sheriff's cousin, Bayton Blankenship, worked as chief investigator for the district attorney's office of that fair city. And me and the sheriff and Bayton had spent one blurry but fun week together deep-sea fishing in Corpus about two years ago. Oh, my, how these things do work out.

I didn't even think about the commissioners as I dialed the long-distance number. After about five minutes of being moved from one sweet-voiced young lady to another, I had Bayton Blankenship on the line.

"Goddamn! Milton Kovak! How you doing?"

"Just fine, Bayton, and yourself?"

"Fine. Fine. How's Elberry doing? Heard about him getting shot. He healing?"

"Yeah, he's giving Miz Blankenship a run for her money. She's having a hell of a time keeping him down."

He laughed. "Well, Elberry knows better than to cross Nadine too much. He'll be good."

"Look, Bayton, the reason I'm calling... I need your help on a little something we got up here."

"Shoot."

"Wonder if you can do some digging for me on a guy named Jerry Johnson. Just background stuff. He lived in Lubbock a long time, as far as I can tell. He's thirty-two years old, if that can help place him some."

"Jerry Johnson? Pretty common name, Milt. This is a big city, not like that little burg you come from."

"Yeah, I understand that. But it sure would help us out up here, Bayton. It surely would."

"Well, you know it's the weekend."

"I need this information before Monday. Life or death."

"Shit. Okay. I'll call you soon as I can."

And I went home and waited. And waited.

SEVENTEEN

SOMEHOW I HAD TO GET Jerry Johnson someplace where Mr. Gilmore could see him and identify him without me pointing at him and saying, "Is that the one?" And also without Jerry Johnson seeing Mr. Gilmore. I didn't want Jerry running at this point.

While I was still thinking about all this, Bayton Blankenship called.

"Milt, got all I can get in this short a time."

"Well, I'll take anything, Bayton."

"Okay, Jerry Johnson was born here in Lubbock. Went to school here, married here. Left about three years ago. Record's clean. Nice, upstanding citizen type. Family man. Any specific questions?"

It was to laugh, so to speak. Nice upstanding citizen. Who had just happened to like to rape and murder little old ladies. I decided to work on Dr. Hutchins' theory. "What about his parents?"

"Hmm…only a mama that I can see, but he wasn't raised by her. Looks like she had him without benefit of marriage, as they say. Her mama raised the boy."

Bingo.

"Okay, Bayton, I sure do appreciate you working on a Saturday and all."

"You owe me, right?" he said and laughed and we said good-bye. Everything was falling into place. All I needed was a witness. That's all I really needed to lock Jerry Johnson up for the rest of his sorry life.

Then it dawned on me that my little escapade of the night before could work for me again. So I called Wayne Swensen and told him that I needed to see each and every one of his salesmen at the station at three o'clock that afternoon. And I called Ervin Gilmore and asked him to be there at two-thirty. Then I went to see the sheriff.

The sheriff insisted on being there, so at two-thirty, he showed up with Mrs. Blankenship's help and sat in his office with Mr. Gilmore, while we waited for the salesmen. Unfortunately, when they got there, I discovered that of the four men, Jerry Johnson was the only one with dark curly hair. So I sent Dalton, who was about Johnson's size, down to the TG & Y to pick up a dark, curly wig, and with Gladys' help, we trimmed it up to look a bit more masculine. Most of the deputies keep a change of clothes at the station, so I had Dalton change into civilian clothes and go into the interrogation room with the salesmen.

At three-thirty we took Mr. Gilmore into the witness room with the two-way mirror and sat him down. He looked at the congregation for only a few seconds before he said, "Oh, Lord. Oh, Lord. It's him." And he wasn't looking at Dalton. He was just standing there, breathing hard and pointing right at Jerry Johnson.

We had Mike take Mr. Gilmore home and the sheriff and I walked into the interrogation room and told all the salesmen they could leave, except Jerry Johnson; we asked him to stay. And then, with me and Dalton as witnesses, the sheriff read him his rights and arrested him for the murder of Mrs. Beatrice Munsky, Mrs. Ida Worth, and the rape of Miss Sue Ellen

Gilmore. I knew in time we'd be playing a tug-of-war over our boy with the other counties and cities where he'd been so god-awful busy, even probably some jurisdictional problems with Texas; but for now, he was all ours.

Jerry Johnson just stood there not looking at anyone. He didn't say a word. Dalton cuffed him and took him off to a holding cell and the sheriff asked him if he wanted us to call somebody from the public defender's office. But still Jerry Johnson didn't say anything.

I told the sheriff I had to leave because I knew I had to get to Laura before this got on the radio. I didn't want her finding out that way. I took the '55 and broke a lot of speed limits getting there, but I figured it didn't matter after what I'd done the night before. And I thought about Laura and the kids and what it would be like on an everyday basis. And how Adam, young as he was, would always think of me as Daddy.

When I pulled up to the crazy house on Mountain Falls Road, the kids were out at the corral, with Laura and Adam watching from the fence. She grabbed Adam and rushed over to the car.

"Did you hear? There was a burglary at Swensen's last night. Jerry's over at the Sheriff's Department now helping out."

"Honey, we got to talk," I said. I waved to the two older kids and took Adam in my arms and led her into the house and into the living room.

"Milt, what is it?"

"Laura, I have something pretty bad I have to tell you."

Her face got pale. "Oh, God. Jerry's been in a wreck."

I shook my head. "No. Honey, we've arrested him for the rape/murders of all those ladies."

She just stood there looking at me for a long moment, then turned her back to me. Softly, almost to herself, I heard her say, "Damn."

And I felt a coldness I'd never felt before. Like a hand had ripped through my shirt, through my skin, grabbed my heart and squeezed it till all the life was gone. Laura knew.

"Laura . . ." I managed to say.

She turned to me but her mind was elsewhere. "Look, Milt, I've got to get a lawyer. I've got a lot of things I need to do."

"You knew, didn't you?"

"What?"

"Why in the hell didn't you stop him? Why didn't you turn the son of a bitch in?"

She looked at me, her eyes big with surprise. "He's my husband, Milt. The father of my children." She said it like a lesson she was teaching one of her children. Just the facts, ma'am.

"Jesus! Little old ladies! That crazy bastard's been murdering innocent little old ladies and you knew!"

Her face turned red and for a minute there she wasn't my beautiful Laura. She was something else entirely. Something I wasn't sure I wanted to know. "Innocent? I'll tell you innocent! Back home in Lubbock one of those sweet little old ladies of yours gave Jerry a case of the clap, which he passed on to me while I was pregnant. And I lost my baby! One of your sweet little old ladies killed my baby!"

"What'd you do, Laura? Go out and buy him the rubbers yourself?" And I knew he hadn't been polite to the old ladies he'd murdered, he'd been polite to his wife.

She didn't say anything, didn't even look at me. "There never was any guy in a green Chevy, was there, Laura?" I asked.

She laughed. A harsh laugh. "For God's sake, Milton, I thought of my two men, you were the grown-up. Don't disappoint me now."

"And us? Was that just your way of keeping tabs on the investigation?"

She shook her head sadly, then looked up at me with those brilliant turquoise eyes. "Maybe. At first. But it sure was nice making love with a man for a change."

I felt a rage I'd never felt before. The baby was heavy in my arms. I looked at sweet little Adam and walked over to the playpen and put him in it.

I looked at Laura and didn't see anything I liked. "I've never hit a woman in my life..."

She laughed. "But you want to hit me, right? Take out all your frustrations on me? How does that make you any different from Jerry?"

She had me there. It didn't. Somewhere in all of us were these demons we either controlled or we didn't. I was lucky. I could control mine.

"Under the law," I said, as steadily as possible, "you're an accessory. Under the law, I should turn you in. But I'm not doing that to those kids. But, Laura, you go on back to Lubbock, you hear? Get out of here now and go on back to Lubbock." I turned away from her and headed for the door. Then turned back. "You got yourself three good little kids here.

Get them some help, okay? They're gonna have a hard time living with what their daddy's done. You take 'em someplace where they can get some help, Laura, you hear me?''

Her once beautiful face was hard. "You leave my kids out of this, Deputy. They're none of your business."

I turned the car around and waved to the kids like it was just any old day. Like it wasn't the end of their lives as they knew them. Like it wasn't the end of mine.

I left and drove back to Longbranch, thinking that if I'd looked into Jerry Johnson early on, the way I'd looked into David Perry and old Stephen P., maybe a couple of old ladies would still be playing with their grandkids. But I hadn't looked into Jerry Johnson, because I never wanted to admit that Laura had a husband. If I didn't look into him, didn't find out about him, then maybe he didn't exist. But he did, and I'd have to live with that somehow.

I pulled into the parking lot of the new building, thinking I was pretty certain who'd be owner number seven of that crazy house as soon as it went on the market, and who'd be spending a lot of time in that windowed room trying not to think about Laura Johnson.

> "Lively and appealing. Simonson deftly juggles a cozy modern suspense story with an up-to-date romance."
>
> —*Publishers Weekly*

LARKSPUR

SHEILA SIMONSON

ODE TO A KILLER

Distinguished poet Dai Llewellyn was throwing his annual summer house party—with the cream of Northern California's literary crop in attendance. Lark Dailey, owner of Larkspur Books, knew four days of bookish chitchat could be tedious—but good for business.

But no sooner had the party come to life when the host died—sipping a glass of Campari laced with a lethal dose of larkspur. Evidently, the killer had a sense of humor. Lark wasn't laughing.

Many had reason to kill the aging poet, whose lauded verse belied a life of sordid affairs and family disharmony. He was also worth millions. Soon, a second, then a third victim appear in this inspired sonnet of death... composed by a clever killer.

HOOKY GETS
THE WOODEN SPOON
LAURENCE MEYNELL

HOOKY HEFFERMAN WAS MUCH BETTER AT GETTING GIRLS IN TROUBLE THAN OUT OF IT.

His passion for the fair sex and English pubs aside, he had been known to solve a crime or two as a private investigator, profiting from the idiocies of this comic adventure called life.

Now he's been hired to find a rebellious, poor little rich girl who has taken up with some unsavory characters. Dad isn't comfortable swimming the murky waters of London's underground. Hooky, however, feels quite at home.

He's never minded helping out a pretty face—and Virginia Chanderley is that—but young and angry, she's also easy prey for a professional crook planning to steal a priceless painting. In fact, lovely Virginia has got herself into more trouble than even Hooky Hefferman—London P.I. and soldier of fortune—knows quite how to handle.

"Laurence Meynell had a gift for creating recognizable characters and ingenious plots."
                                                        —*The Independent*

THE CRUEL MOTHER

First Time in Paperback

A MEG HALLORAN MYSTERY

JANET LAPIERRE

WERE THEY CAPTIVES BECAUSE OF SOME MOUNTAIN MAN'S FANTASY? OR SOMETHING COMPLETELY UNCONNECTED?

Meg Halloran's romantic getaway with longtime love, policeman Vince Gutierrez looks less appealing when Vince reluctantly introduces the third member of their party, his spike-haired, foul-mouthed niece, Cass.

An accident with another car abruptly ends their plans. Then Meg and Cass are inexplicably abducted, held in a secluded wilderness cabin in Idaho's panhandle.

Meg desperately seeks answers—and a means of escape—unaware her fate lies with strangers: a terminally-ill sixties radical who recently confessed to murder; his wife, emerging from seclusion to reunite the dying man with their young daughter; and a lawyer, calculating one of the biggest scores of his circumspect career....

MYSTERY **WORLDWIDE LIBRARY**

MARY KITTREDGE
DEAD AND GONE

First Time in Paperback

A CHARLOTTE KENT MYSTERY

DEADLINES

When writer Charlotte Kent began researching her latest self-help book, *Tricks for the Sick!* at a renowned East Coast medical center, she hadn't planned a chapter on tips to avoid murder.

A slimy, unprincipled medical student is dead. His wife, a friend of Charlotte's, is the prime suspect. But Charlotte, with her stubborn yen for justice and an unerring nose for the messiest sort of problems, believes otherwise.

Problem one: the body has disappeared from the morgue. Problem two: it seems the victim had his unscrupulous fingers in some heavy-duty blackmail. Problem three: her chief suspect is the medical center's richest, most-respected doctor.

For this hustling, hump-it-to-the-deadline free-lance writer, the final chapter was going to be the killer.

"Charlotte Kent is a truly engaging amateur sleuth."

—*Publishers Weekly*

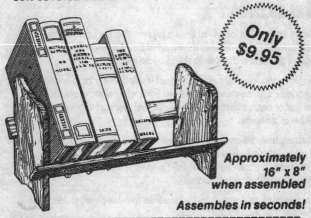